THE ALPHA'S FAKE MATE

The Omega Misfits Book #2

by

Wendy Rathbone

For Della, as always...

Chapter One

Holland

The water in the old pool with the chipped tiles at the edges made lapping sounds as the filter turned on. I sat in a lounge chair pressed up against the chain link fence and watched the sky turn purple beyond the farm's Children's Wing.

All the familiar night sounds hadn't changed: the wind in the pines that said summer was ending, the clatter and voices from the dining hall as dinner was prepared, and far-off, the ghostly voice of an owl calling its mate.

Nothing had changed, really. The concrete at my feet was pock-marked from too many seasons. The chlorine scent stung my nose. And I was still an Omega through and through with no right to speak of what had happened to me, and no recourse to receive justice in any definition of that word.

I shut my eyes tight in an effort to block it all out. But that only made sensations and images spark clearer in my memory.

Mean hands clenched to fists spinning all around.

A laughing growl of a voice: "You can't run away."

The clash of teeth everywhere tender that could be reached.

The Alpha didn't want to just fuck me, he wanted to tear me apart. His Burn made him want to see me bleed and scream. He liked that sound. It took him into euphoria.

"The way the blood looks purple against your skin," he'd said to me. "So beautiful."

With him, my moments of consciousness grew fewer.

I knew I would die, my screams unheard, no one coming to help.

Alphas in the Burn might lose their minds. We'd been taught this. But here on Zilly's chattel farm the Alphas they brought in for the eighteens and older weren't labeled dangerous. There were other private establishments for that crazy-Alpha kind of behavior. We serviced the Alphas who just needed to get through their Burns with an easy companion.

It was safe for us here. We were raised to be with them in their Burns, built for it. It was our duty.

That was what my teachers said. What they taught.

My friends who turned eighteen before me and had their first times said it wasn't terrible. Most liked it. Most got off on it.

My best friend Harly had a great first time. He came back from the mating hall all flushed and contented, wearing a sliver-moon smile. "I'm ready to go again, now," he had said. "Holland, you have nothing to be scared of. It's natural, after all. What we're born to do."

But I was the nervous type. Kids laughed when I jumped at a sudden sound or recoiled at an unexpected touch. Unlike my friends, I didn't partake in certain physical acts my peers did at puberty, sneaking around with each other after lights out, making each other sigh and moan.

It was against the rules and I was sort of a nerd about the rules. Besides, if you were caught fucking around, or if the contraceptives didn't work and you got pregnant, they sent you off somewhere Omegas got punished. Maybe to the farms where the dangerous Alphas went. Or maybe even to prison.

Omegas weren't supposed to fuck each other. Ever. If the contraceptives didn't work and you got pregnant, you'd give birth to a monster. A Sylph. No one wanted that. Sylphs were abominations, raised in institutions to keep the population safe from them. They were crazy, wild beings, and if they lived through puberty they suffered the Burn all the time with no relief. They had to be shut away in isolation forever.

"At least we have it better than a Sylph," Harly always said. "We get our needs taken care of here, we get to have hot sex, and maybe one day a rich nice Alpha will mate-bond us and we can go off our contraceptives and have a family."

When I turned eighteen, six months after Harly, it should have been an exciting day for me. I was finally an adult. We were trained it was a gift to lose our virginity to an Alpha, which was why we must remain pure and not be tempted by each other.

I listened. Most did not. But I did. I tried to believe. I was a virgin when my birthday arrived.

But that day, though it started out sunny with a cake baked for me by Nod, our old Omega house-dad, soon became a nightmare.

Now I watched the sky darken. I heard the bell for supper. But I didn't want any.

I raised my bandaged arm to my face, flexing my fingers. My wrist was broken, and two knuckles on my other hand were fractured. I pushed my dark bangs back and blinked upward, looking for the first star.

Six days I had not seen the stars. I'd spent one half hour servicing the violent Alpha that had been trying to kill me until an Omega mating hall monitor heard my faint screams through the walls and checked in on us. The six nights afterward I had spent in the hospital.

The monitor had had to gas the room to get the Alpha to stop strangling me. The gas was part of an emergency system in place if an Alpha ever got out of control. I'd never heard of it being used. During the Burn, most Alphas, even if they got a little rambunctious, could still be reasoned with.

I swallowed roughly, the bruises on my neck pressing my shirt collar.

I heard a door bang open.

"Hey, Holland! There you are. Dinner's on! What are you doing out here? Are you all right?"

Of course I wasn't all right and he knew it.

Harly came up to me, his sweet face surrounded by blond curls. "Do you need help with your crutch?"

"No. I got it."

Harly had visited me every day while I was in the hospital. He'd put on his happy face and never let up. It made my stomach churn, but I said nothing. He was my friend. I knew he hated that I'd been hurt. He was the type who wanted to put any bad thing behind him and never talk or think about it.

He watched me struggle up with my bum leg and arm, and my aching muscles, as I got my crutch under me. I could only use a crutch for one side. My broken wrist wouldn't hold me if I used it to support myself on a second crutch.

"How long have you been out here?" he asked.

"I don't know."

Even though I said no to his offer of help, he still put his arm around my waist and let me lean my weight on him as he walked with me to the dining hall.

We sat side by side in the adult section now. My trial by fire had earned me my adult status. But it hurt to sit. I angled to one side for more comfort. No one brought me a pillow, or even seemed to notice. I knew they didn't want to notice because it could have been any of them in my place. It still could be. If Alphas were not properly vetted, dangerous ones could slip through here on the farm at any time. They didn't teach that in our health and sexuality classes.

Old Omegas who had never been mate-bonded served us our dinner. Nod, who I had known my whole life, was a hundred and fifty years old. He still had a good fifty years left in him. He brought me my tray special. He set it in front of me and said, "Take your pills now and you'll get better faster."

There were three big pills, green, yellow and white, sitting on the tray by my silverware. One of them was a pain pill. I got them twice a day.

I nodded, looking down at my food. I wasn't hungry but I knew if I took the pills without food I'd have a stomach ache later.

While Harly made light, casual banter with our friends at the table, I forced the food down my throat. It wasn't bad food. Omegas were great cooks. But my body had become frozen since my ordeal, cold and shuddery. I didn't know how to make that stop. Maybe it would always be that way now. No matter how many blankets I used I would always be cold. No matter how tightly I clenched my muscles, I would always shake.

I focused on getting the food down, tasting sawdust. Half-way through the meal, Warden Chirl, who often walked about the dining hall checking in with everyone, stopped by my side.

"I'd like to see you in my office after dinner."

Harly looked up with wide eyes.

"Yes, sir," I said.

Chirl wore the black robe of his distinguished designation, placing him in a higher rank above us all. It was belted in gold. The house-dads, cooks and old servants all dressed in white robes with a hemp braid about their waists. The fresh Omegas who serviced Alphas (of which I was one now) wore white-collared shirts and loose black trousers. The kids were outfitted in blue jumpsuits.

"I'll make sure he gets there," Harly said helpfully, nodding at Chirl.

"Thank you, Harly," said Chirl.

When the warden left, Harly spoke aside to me. "He'll make everything better. You'll see."

We all trusted Warden Chirl. Or, at least, I had until my first mating.

Now I trusted no one. Not even chipper, smiling Harly.

I turned away from him and poked at my food, wishing the pain pill would work faster. My injuries were healing quickly, but in the meantime I battled.

I had bite marks all over my body, including my cock, which the doctors treated and promised would leave no scars. I had bruised ribs, a broken wrist and a sprained ankle, and a still raspy throat with severe bruising from almost being choked to death. My ass had been abraded but left to heal on its own without stitches.

"You were lucky," one of the doctors had said to me.

Yeah. Right.

It wasn't pretty. And I wasn't going to be smiling any time soon.

*

After dinner, Harly stayed by my side as I hobbled and stumbled my way down the long hall to the warden's office on my single crutch.

When the door to the office closed behind me, Warden Chirl stood from behind his big oak desk and motioned for me to sit. Luckily, the chair facing him was plush leather, and soft. I almost sighed as I sank into it.

"Holland, how are you feeling today?" he asked gently.

"Better." My voice came out raw and low.

Chirl had visited me twice in the hospital, his face wearing worried expressions. Both times when he turned to leave, I saw he held his hands behind his back so tightly they were bone white in color.

I knew there were things he wasn't telling me, perhaps things he could never say. While the Alpha doctors and nurses seemed more worried about my beauty not being permanently marred, Chirl had my emotional well-being in mind. It swirled in his eyes and showed in those tightly clasped hands.

It was a good thing I'd been so out of it for those days, or I would have panicked every time an Alpha doctor or nurse touched me. Though they were gentle and professional always, frankly I never wanted to see another Alpha again.

"The doctors inform me you will heal perfectly. You will be fine. This is good news."

"I guess."

I looked down at my hands in my lap. My wrist and forearm was wrapped tight in a thick cast, the other hand decorated with two splints for my broken fingers. They were my littlest fingers, which was why I could still use the crutch with that hand.

"But the doctors do not take into account injuries and scars that cannot be seen."

I closed my eyes and saw the blood well up in the carpet of the mating room. The memory of his terrible voice said, "Pretty little thing not so pretty anymore."

Chirl brought me back to reality. "I'm going to recommend our Omega therapist, Sen. You'll be seeing him once a day at first."

I started to shake my head no.

"This is not up for discussion," Chirl continued.

I lifted my head, my bangs dark in my eyes. "What would there be to talk about?"

"Well, for one thing, can you integrate back into the Omega population here on the farm?"

My heart seemed to stop. "What does that mean? If I don't, you'll send me away?"

"No, no, not at all. Shhh."

I didn't realize until then that I'd raised my voice to him.

But who cared? I needed to be blunt now. What had happened was a crime but no one was going to pay for it but me.

"But you are saying if I can't be psychologically conditioned to go back to servicing Alphas again that my options are limited."

"You can remain here."

"Right. To serve Omegas?"

Like the others, I had hoped to one day find my mate and have a happy mate-bond. I never had a single thought I'd spend the rest of my life serving other Omegas like Nod and the other cooks and house-dads did. Like Chirl himself, though he wore the black robes of rank which meant he made a salary and possibly even had a real bank account.

"Yes."

I'd had dreams, even if they were shitty Omega dreams. I'd hoped maybe an Alpha would love me and want to form the mate-bond. Maybe I'd have children one day and be able to watch them grow and learn.

"What other future could there be for me?"

"If you heal well, there is still the possibility of a mate."

But I knew he lied. I was ruined if I couldn't make myself go back to the mating hall.

"I don't see that being possible now." I kept my voice low and flat. "I won't go back to the mating hall. But I don't want to spend my life serving Omegas, either."

"That's why I want you to see the therapist."

"Whatever."

Chirl let my snarky comment pass. "You need time to heal and I'm giving it to you. Time off from your classes, your chores and your mating hall duties. If, in three months, you find you cannot go back to the hall duty, we'll reassess then."

He was being as fair as he could be to me, but there really was no justice. Not for the crime against me. Not for me.

The fury inside me boiled. The edges of my vision went red. I would never go back to the hall duties. I knew that. But I kept my mouth shut.

Chirl came out from behind his desk and put his palm against my shoulder as he handed me a card. "Your appointment is with Sen. Three o'clock every day for a week at first. Then every other day."

Sen. I'd only glimpsed him around the farm but I'd never had to see him in any official capacity. There were over a thousand of us here including the under eighteens, but they mostly stayed in the children's wing. It was like living in a small town, I guess. Faces became familiar over a lifetime, but we didn't all know each other.

Sen had been around since I could remember. He was like a counselor for us, along with a few others on staff. I'd never needed his service. His reputation was okay but beyond that I knew nothing about him. And I wasn't keen on learning.

Omegas could not become real doctors, but Omegas could take classes online and get certified in lesser degrees. Sen was one. A psychologist. If we Omegas ever needed an M.D. for any reason, we had to see Alphas for that.

Chirl pressed my shoulder. "You will make sure you make the appointment."

I nodded once, staring at my lap.

"Good."

I glanced up quickly, tightening the muscles around my eyes. "Are we done?"

"For now." Chirl stepped back as I rose.

Half-way to the door, his voice followed me. "I'm sorry this happened to you, Holland. You're not the first. You won't be the last."

"It is what it is," I muttered.

"Come to me if you need anything."

I need to not be here in the first place. But I didn't say that thought aloud.

I didn't turn back. I didn't thank him. I kept going until the door slammed at my back and I stood, sweating and pissed, in the empty corridor.

Maybe he saw my behavior as rude. I didn't care.

I only wanted to be far away from my Omega status, this place, the world. I was as trapped in my life as any animal pacing the length of its cage. There was no way out for me.

Chapter Two

Orion

"Sign here, and here. And here." The attorney pointed to the yellow highlighted lines.

The pen in my hand was thick and smooth, black with a gold tip and cap. I swirled my Os. I took my time with the curls of my signature.

Just a few more precious seconds of bought time seemed like nothing, but to me every delay meant one more day, one more minute without having to think. To be responsible.

But today everything changed. The minutes rushed by too fast, like lights on the highway, the traffic surging, everything in a hurry.

I had just gotten my degree in microbiology, which did nothing for me unless I wanted to go to med school, or do research.

I no longer needed to do either, though. I had a new career.

My friends said I was lucky. I'd just inherited sixty-five point seven million dollars, after taxes, from my Alpha dad whom I had not seen since I'd gone off to the academy against his will. He'd wanted me to stay behind and go into business with him. But I hated his business.

Now it was mine, along with all the money it generated.

I leaned forward in my chair, elbow on the attorney's desk, and ran my fingers through my bangs, pushing upward, tugging hard. "Now. What do I have to do to sell that?"

I pointed to the paper I had just signed that wasn't cash, but assets. One in particular. An inherited asset I wanted nothing to do with.

"Sell that one?" he asked. "Why would you do such a thing? It's a cash cow. You may have money now, but this business guarantees you're set for life should the worst happen, should banks fail or the other businesses dry up."

"I don't want to be responsible for it."

"You have everything set into place. And an agency that runs it for you. You need do nothing and the cash flows in. Orion, why would you sell?"

Most Alphas would not understand. But then most Alphas didn't give a shit what happened to Omegas who were out of their sight. My dad was one of them. He had no conscience about his business practices, and if unsavory things happened, he signed off on them and let others handle the fallout.

I wasn't my dad. I was the type of kid who couldn't just let things slide. I got into a lot of fights as a teen not because I was a bully, but because I could not tolerate bullies.

Alphas will be Alphas, so the saying goes. Aggression and strength were rewarded. We who were richer were even more privileged. We ran the world with no consequence to bad behavior. Asserting power and authority over others for fun was considered a positive trait, even if it hurt them. Short of murder, Alpha bullies were considered winners in life.

Maybe hating my dad fed my ire. When I grew big enough to take the assholes of my grade, the more popular Alphas in my private school avoided me. But nothing changed. Not the actions of Alphas, or the school, or the whole wide planet.

I could only affect my own little area of the world, quietly getting my science degree and slaking my Burns at privately vetted Omega cloisters where Omegas had the most rights and could accept or decline a customer at will, and where I knew they would not freak out over an Alpha who might want a less than submissive partner for a couple of days.

My dad paid for everything without a word.

Now, all my dad owned had become mine.

The attorney poured more wine into my glass, then helped himself. It seemed wrong to drink it under such bright fluorescents which illuminated the paperwork that bragged of such obscene wealth. Wrong to celebrate, somehow.

He leaned forward, bringing his face more in line with my own.

"If you want to sell," he said. "All right. But don't you think you should have a look first at what you're giving up? If you don't like something, you certainly have the money to make changes."

I sighed. "Maybe."

"Basically, if you sell, you lose all control. Who knows what the new owner might do to the place? But if you keep it, you can maintain it the way you like. Not your father's way, but your way. Maybe even better than the way your father ran it."

I touched the now dried ink of my signature on the last form. "Zilly's. I don't even know why it's called that. I never wanted anything to do with the farms. Maybe because my dad owned one. But now I don't know what to do."

"I'll set up a tour. See what you think. If you want to liquidate afterward, I'll put that into motion. But my opinion is it's worth more to keep it than to sell."

I gave in to him for two reasons. One, because he'd made a convincing argument, and two, because I was somewhat curious.

Just the idea of chattel farms made me cringe. My attorney was right, though. If I kept ownership I would have control. I could choose hands off or hands on. I could make sure the Omegas were treated with decency at the very least.

Most Alphas might look down on Omegas as second class citizens, but experience I'd had with the ones I'd met taught me they were as smart and capable as we were. Their statures, for the most part, might be smaller, their faces softer and prettier, their scents sweet as fresh cut flowers, but the look in their eyes was as fierce and intelligent and determined as any Alpha I had known. Somehow, in some warped and

15

broken way, someone deep in the past had decided because Omegas had egg sacks and produced lubricant making them eager to be penetrated, they were less than us, unequal because they were submissive.

I knew though, that if you really studied submissive behavior in animals, you could see the one on the bottom was the one in charge, and if a mating had to be forced, where did that get fun?

But talk like that could get you bad grades in biology class, not to mention a life without friends.

The attorney—I guess he was now my attorney, Mister Saben Tratto, Esquire JD—brought up his tablet and started scrolling through it.

"I can set up a tour with you and the board for Thursday next week," he said.

I didn't need to check my own calendar. It was empty. I couldn't decide if I wanted to go back to school or not for a PhD. I had money now, so I thought about doing some traveling first. Go skiing in the Alps. Maybe buy a boat. Or a giraffe for the huge front yard of my dad's house which was now my house. Wasn't that what rich men did?

"Thursday will be fine."

"Good. We'll all meet out front of Zilly's at three."

We both rose at the same time. Saben shook my hand.

"You're a wealthy man now. You keep that farm and let it continue to do business, and you'll grow even wealthier."

Well, I would think about it, at least.

In the parking lot, I got into my Jeep. My dad had left me his Rolls and his Porsche and his limo and driver. But I still loved my Jeep.

I sat in the sun-warmed seat for a few minutes doing nothing. I had just inherited multi-millions, and an Omega chattel farm I didn't want. But I didn't feel like much had changed. That was probably because I'd already had everything I wanted in life. What a privileged ass I was!

I should be celebrating. My dad had died a year ago, so there was no sadness. Even then, when I'd gotten word of the plane crash, I hadn't cried. Not one salty tear.

Finally, I decided to text some of my college buddies. We'd all just graduated. Many of them were in between more schooling or jobs.

I invited them to dinner at the best steakhouse in the city. My treat.

Every one of them accepted the invite.

Chapter Three

Holland

I kicked at the thick, beige carpet.

I'd gotten the brace off my ankle yesterday, and it was still sore. I didn't care.

"It gets us nowhere to hate ourselves," said Sen.

"I never said I hated myself."

"Yet you want to die."

"To escape."

"That would only be hurting yourself."

"Why would I want to hurt myself? Or hate myself? I'm a good person. I've never done anything wrong. I haven't harmed others. It's the world I hate, but I can't kill the world, now, can I?"

Sen had this irritating mint habit. The air was filled with wintergreen. He sucked on his candies throughout each of our sessions. It was a wonder he still had all his teeth.

He was a gangly guy with a craggy, but still handsome face, and his smile showed slightly yellowed but perfect teeth. I never asked him his age, but I figured somewhere between seventy and a hundred.

"I'm not going to hurt myself," I confessed with a deep exhale. "But fuck this. I am not going back to the mating halls. And I hate to cook! I'm not going to spend my life in service to other Omegas."

"It hasn't been long enough for you to make any decisions. We need to focus on emotional health at this time, how to make you feel good about yourself again."

It had been two months already. Nothing was improving except my body, which healed rather quickly without a care to my mental state.

"I feel just fine!" I argued. Some part of me, even before the attack, had always been slightly contrary. But certainly I did feel fine. Physically, I was healed. Mentally, I knew nothing about this fucking situation had been my fault and I resented it more every day.

And the anger. I hated everyone and everything. Even Harly couldn't get me to do much. Play games with him and the others? That was kid shit. I mostly kept to myself and read or watched vids.

"You may think you feel fine," Sen said. "But you aren't ready to be making any decisions right now about what you may be willing to do or not do."

"I won't go back to the mating hall ever again, I know that." I folded my arms in front of me.

"Like anyone your age, you don't dream to be mate-bonded?"

"Did you?" I shot back, knowing he was un-mated and alone. Knowing I was being rude.

Calmly, Sen replied. "I did. It never happened for me. None found me compatible."

I lowered my eyelids. "I'm sorry."

"Don't be. Not all Omegas need an Alpha to feel complete."

I sat straighter. "You believe that?"

He nodded.

"Maybe I could get more schooling. Like you did."

"It's rare for Omegas to be accepted into higher learning programs, even online ones. Half don't ever graduate."

"Yeah, because they get pregnant, or told they're dumb or something. I know all that."

"There's nothing wrong with falling in love. Nothing wrong with getting pregnant."

"Yeah? Well I don't believe in love. Everything's hormones and chemicals. It's not real."

"Have you always believed that way?"

Stupid question. I didn't want to answer because thinking about my former dreams hurt too much. Whenever I looked at my past self and my childhood hopes, I saw rubble.

"You're not going to answer that question? Or you can't?"

"I can."

Sen waited.

"I was naïve. Just like all the others. What you teach us here, it's wrong. Do you ever have a conscience about that?"

Sen leaned forward. "What happened to you is a crime. It's not a normal occurrence. You can only see your world through that filter now, and no one is blaming you for that. All I can do is make you aware of that fact. I can't heal you. I can, however, assist you in healing yourself. You may never be ready or you may be ready tomorrow, but I am here for you."

Here for me. Every other day now. It was his job. It was bullshit.

I looked up at the clock on the wall above shelves of musty, old-looking books. Four minutes and our time would be up. I was counting them down. I wanted to leave.

Our sessions felt useless to me. Sure, Sen was nice. His words and advice made sense. My rational self understood them clearly. But I couldn't make my deeper self abide. I couldn't stop the pure outrage that ruled me even in my sleep when I would startle awake and stare at the darkness for hours, unable to find peace.

After the attack, how could I not hate what I was? And all Omegas, for that matter. How could they continue to be meek and take only what was offered, and accept their subservient roles as if nature intended it?

The attack not only changed me, it woke me. I didn't know if I could ever go back to sleep and trudge through this world as a breeder, a servant and nothing more.

I heard Sen talking but it was all a background drone to my unending anger. A few times, Sen tried to make me understand my anger as grief.

"Grief for what?" I'd asked.

"All you have lost."

"What did I ever have in the first place?" I had replied.

No. Sen would never make me see anger as grief. Because it wasn't. I was outraged, insulted and demoralized. I had been tortured and almost died.

What grief?

Sometimes I questioned his degree that hung in a gold frame on the wall behind where he sat at his desk. Sometimes I wondered if an Alpha therapist might be a better fit. I wouldn't feel guilty when I yelled and lashed out. He would be a good target for me to rage against.

I might hate all Omegas now, but I still felt guilty if I blamed them for my hate. It was as if I were betraying my own kind.

But not so with Alphas.

I glanced again at the big analog clock on the wall. Its second hand slowly swept the face past the four and the five. Two and half more minutes.

"Holland."

I glanced up. "What?"

"Did you hear me?"

"Hear what?"

Sen sighed. "It can wait until your next session in two days. I know you're tired."

"I'm not tired." My contrariness came from deep within. A place I'd kept secret and buried, going along with the flow and the crowd, not making waves as I'd been taught. Then that Alpha monster breached through all my barriers using fear, pain and cruel ridicule to break me. Maybe I wasn't changed so much as stripped of all ideals and rules I'd once held close, false or not. They had comforted me.

No comfort remained for me now.

I glanced up at the clock. Thirty more seconds.

Sen said, "All right then. Our time is up for the day."

I got to my feet slowly. My body had healed but residual aches remained. I was allowed one ibuprofen every eight hours, doled out by Chirl. It wasn't quite enough but took the edge off.

The hallway smelled of pine. Someone had just mopped but the floor was mostly dry, and sparkled.

I heard a bunch of voices in the front room, out of sight. It sounded almost like a party. A party I wasn't invited to.

I'd stayed to myself all day. I had grabbed a breakfast sandwich early in the morning and eaten it in my room, then skipped lunch. So if anything was going on today with those who weren't serving in the mating hall, I wouldn't have known it.

I wasn't in the mood for company, let alone a party, but curiosity got the better of me. Instead of turning back to my room and my videos and books, I headed toward the dozens of hushed voices all talking at once.

Footsteps clattered down the hall behind me. I turned to see who it was. Harly glided by me, slowing only to grab my hand. "Come on!" he said.

I pulled my hand back with a hard tug. "What?"

He shrugged and moved on, shaking his head. We hadn't been on good terms lately and it was my fault. I hadn't talked to him in days, as well as preferring to eat alone.

I followed him at a slow walk and when I saw the big front room filled with Omegas, some from my class and some older, I couldn't figure it out. They lined up in rows against the walls, looking neat and tidy in their white shirts and black trousers. The Omega staff stood by the entrance in their white robes. Warden Chirl, in his distinguished black, headed the group.

Frowning, I strained around the corner to see what they were all looking at.

The double doors to the front of the building opened and in walked a group of suited men, all tall, all broad-shouldered.

Alphas!

My body stiffened in immediate shock. A fear response I couldn't control sent cold needle-like threads into my veins.

22

Alphas never came into our living spaces. Never. In my lifetime, I'd never heard of it. They were allowed only in the mating hall, and in special meeting rooms if they wanted to court a claim on a specific Omega. Where we lived and were raised was supposed to be an Alpha-free safe zone.

"What?"

Harly, standing about three feet in front of me, turned to look at me. "I count six. I didn't think it would be that many."

"What is the meaning of this?"

A hush fell over the room and only then did I realize I'd yelled the words.

"Why the fuck are they in here!" I yelled.

The Alphas all stopped talking and glanced through the crowd in my direction. My Omega peers all turned to look at me, too.

Harly touched my arm. "Shhh! Don't be rude! They're invited."

My eyes burned. I kept gulping air as a chill came over me at getting everyone's attention.

I wanted to run but I couldn't move. It was as if time had stopped and I was paralyzed, able to see but not comprehend. I leaned back, feeling the hardness of the wall behind me for support. Darkness threatened the edges of my vision.

The tallest Alpha of the six, and the youngest and most handsome, raised both eyebrows as he stared at me. An older Alpha with gray at his temples leaned in to speak to him.

Warden Chirl nodded as if he heard what was said. "You're welcome here." He held out his arms in an open gesture.

The Alphas continued forward into the room, into our safe space.

More nods. More forced smiles. All the attention that was turned onto me seconds ago reverted back to the six intruders.

But the young Alpha kept staring at me and I couldn't breathe. I couldn't think. All I could feel was danger. But in reality, these Alphas acted as normal as anyone.

Chirl turned and spoke to the room.

"The new owner of Zilly's has come today to tour our farm. Now, he is the owner which means he has free reign. You are to show these men all courtesy and assist them if they have questions."

The young Alpha's eyes flashed and his jaw firmed as he dropped his gaze from mine and took in the room.

"Hello," he said.

His voice a deep rumble, rich and strong, vibrated the air and tumbled straight through me. My mouth went dry.

"My name is Orion. Now I know I'm new and this usually isn't done this way, but I want to assure you all I am here to assess this farm as a whole. I've never been here before, and if improvements need to be made, as well as updates to your living conditions, I want to hear about it. Your house-dads have surveys to pass around to you all. I hope you fill them out. I intend to read each and every one."

A new owner! What if he didn't like what he saw? What would happen to us?

The way he lorded himself! At such a young age, what would he know about anything yet? He was obviously unbonded, like a lot of Alphas who preferred to remain that way and treat Omegas only as breeders for their young, keeping the Alpha babies and shipping Omegas off to be raised on the farms.

His stupid survey was a ruse, I was sure. To keep us in line. To learn how better he could control his new asset. Not for one minute did I think he would spend any of his own precious money to make life for us here an improvement over what it was: to be chattel for Alphas in the Burn. We were primed and programmed since infancy to be sold for sex, and there was no other way to sugar coat it.

I watched my house-mates stand tall, some even combing their hair back with their fingers, primping and preening for the pack of Alphas now invading our private space. When before I might have gone with the flow, pushing down my secret resentment, now it all came flooding out.

My rage made me dizzy.

When the Alpha Orion was done giving his speech, smiling with his perfect white teeth, wavy brown hair glistening with gold streaks in the light, his gaze sought me again.

I nearly hissed as I gave him my worst glare. My breaths came fast.

His brow furrowed. His head tilted. One of the other Alphas put a hand on the center of his back and his body stiffened, the muscles bunching under his suit blazer, tugging at the arms and shoulders.

He was a big one. At least six-three.

What was he seeing that made him keep looking at me? A pathetic human who couldn't care for himself? A lowly Omega who dared meet his gaze? Prey?

My palms pressed hard against the cool wall behind me, grounding me.

The Alpha turned away. He approached Chirl and said something low that I couldn't hear.

Warden Chirl looked in my direction, then replied. All I heard were murmurs and the heavy breathing around me of excited Omegas all dreaming of bondmates and children and rich Alphas sweeping them off their feet.

All stupid idiots.

What was Chirl saying to him? Something about me?

The Alpha glanced up at me again for a split-second, then turned and accompanied his group as Chirl showed them around the front room and into the dining hall. Some Omegas followed at a discreet distance.

My heart hammered in my chest. Flashback images came to me again of my first meeting with an Alpha, how he grabbed me, twisted me, punched, bit and defiled for his own pleasure. I had thought I would at least respond to his smell, feel an urge biologically, but he had no scent I could discern other than a burnt sweaty smell that filled me with fear. Everything he did hurt me and he didn't care.

As I watched the Alphas leave the room, the youngest one, the new owner, turned back one more time to look at me.

The muscles of my face hardened. My teeth gritted. I turned and ran down the spotless, shining hallway toward the back door that led to the private pool area.

Under a slatted awning, in darker shadows, I found my favorite lounge chair and sat. I stared at the lapping blue water, listened to the pump and breathed in the faint chlorine scent that I'd come to associate with comfort.

I shut my eyes and tried to focus back in time to my childhood when I was not aware of how the world worked. When I was happier.

Chapter Four

Orion

I thought Zilly's would be more run-down and depressing. More desolate, I guess.

But as I walked in with Saben and other Alpha staff who oversaw the finances and farm upkeep, I saw clean lines, polished floors and open windows letting in lots of sunlight.

I had a stereotype in my head that it would be more like an Omega workhouse from the early nineteen-hundreds or something. Maybe I'd been watching too many early historical films when I was young. I'm not sure what formed that image in my head and made me want to avoid the farms during my Burns. It could all boil down to the fact that my dad owned one and he had always been so cold.

The Omegas that greeted us were healthy and held their heads high. The ones who ran the place were intelligent and friendly. I'd expected them to be hideous, perhaps, because they were unbonded, but there it was again. My own ignorance and shallow views.

One Omega, however, caught my eye. A stunning boy, he could not have been more than nineteen. He stood back from the crowd near a hallway, tense and unhappy. No, not unhappy. Furious.

I noticed him because he, out of all of them, did not have himself under control. Nor was he at all interested in being polite.

"What is the meaning of this?" he shouted. "What are you all doing here?"

His hair was swept to one side and spread dark and mirror-shiny over his right cheek. His white shirt fit loosely at his lean waist, and crumpled at the waistband of his black trousers. His features were angular and beautiful, delicate and sharp at the same time, like some fairy tale elf from a fantasy book cover.

He fumed, huffing and almost growling at us.

He was insanely beautiful.

He held my gaze as if ready to do battle. Here in this clean and well-lighted place where everyone seemed fairly content if not happy, he was the only one who exhibited any animosity. If looks really could kill, I would have been twitching on the floor, gasping my last breath.

After he'd made his statements, I leaned forward as Warden Chirl apologized for him.

"I'm sorry for that. He's suffered trauma and is still recovering," the Omega whispered. "My apologies for his outburst."

"What has happened to him?"

Chirl shook his head as if to tell me later.

I respected his wishes, but the matter was haunting. Here I had seen everything so clean and perfect, and this dark presence left a stain. I didn't blame the Omega, but I wanted to know why. Every place had its secrets. An Omega farm would be no exception to that rule. Call me a control freak, but since I now owned the place, I wanted in on all the secrets.

I kept looking back at him, the brooding Omega now pressed against the back wall, as if he might suddenly reveal some answer. Or produce another outburst.

Of course it only made his mystery deepen as he thinned his lips and continued to glare.

Warden Chirl guided us through double doors to another part of the complex. I finally turned to follow, but as I did, I saw out the corner of my eye the angry Omega turn away and run down the hall out of sight. He limped slightly, his uneven footsteps echoing before I realized I hadn't heard a word Chirl had said after his whispered apology. The blood rushed in my ears.

I'd never had such a response to an Omega before, neither in nor out of the Burn. Was it the challenge the angry one presented? Or my curiosity about what made him look so painfully furious? Or was it simply his ethereal beauty that brought out my shallow side?

"This way, Orion," Saben, my lawyer, said.

I blinked. I'd wandered away from the group without noticing and now faced a blurred painting on a wall. It was of wheat blowing in a wind, the sun shining on it from a low angle, the sky turning pink above.

The artist had captured the movement of the weather in the picture exquisitely.

"An Omega did this?" I asked, pretending I'd been distracted by the painting this whole time.

"Yes." Chirl came toward me. "A twelfth year from ten years ago. He's mate-bonded now, with three children of his own."

"He's very talented. Does he continue to paint?"

"I don't know."

Those three words made a hollow sort of chill begin to form in my chest. A talented man had done this and no one knew if he'd continued to paint or not. As an Omega, he probably would not be given any space to show his work. So why would he bother to continue?

No, he'd mate-bonded and was now raising a family. That was his reason for living now. That was what Omegas did, while Alphas controlled everything from business to art to deciding who they would or would not breed with.

My mind kept going back to that angry boy. Zilly's seemed like a decent place where Omegas were educated, given a healthy life, and yet it made its profit—my profit now—by selling Omega services to Alphas in the Burn.

While I'd been taught that was the nature of things, and Omegas were always eager to please, I'd be stupid to think there wasn't a darker side, that there would be Omegas who could not fit in, who were unable to give in to their natures, or who were simply unhappy.

Was this business one I really wanted to keep? I didn't need the money so I wasn't forced to take a profit off people who had no choice in their fates.

While I was being shown around by the warden who openly answered all our questions, I wondered how I could find out about the things I didn't know to ask. I wanted to talk to that boy. The bright and happy Omegas, eager to please, could offer only one side to life here at Zilly's. I wanted to see the writing on the pages not so easily turned.

After a time, Chirl and his associates led us outdoors to the beautiful grounds of the farm. A sloping, well-manicured lawn, at least ten acres back, led to a line of old pines that brushed the sky in a high, soft wind. A fountain trickled nearby. I heard it before I saw it: Two five foot tall stone lions on their hind legs grappled. Water came out of their mouths and poured into a pond green with lily pads. White flowers bloomed across the small body of water, scenting the air.

Beyond the fountain was a blacktop area with basketball hoops, and beyond that a sandy area with volleyball nets.

These Omegas certainly got exercise and fresh air. My dad had not allowed this place to become run-down as I had feared.

Chirl saw my gaze and said, "There's a pool, too. It's a good size but not huge, so in the summer we put the boys in groups to take their turns at swimming lessons and recreation. Everyone here knows how to swim."

"And you have an indoor gym, too, you said." I wanted confirmation. Everything seemed almost too good to be true.

"Yes."

"Would it be all right if I had a look around out here? By myself, I mean. I'd just like to get a feel for things. Walk down to those pines." I felt that Chirl was rushing us through this tour.

"Of course. You are free to move about, except the dorms where I will accompany you, and that's only because they are personal living spaces."

"I understand. I won't wander in there unaccompanied, I promise."

There were benches around the fountain and lily pond. I left my group there with Saben, who questioned me with his eyebrows.

I shook my head at him.

I heard Chirl order one of his men to bring drinks. Lemonade. Perfect for a nice autumn day like this. But I didn't want lemonade. I knew I couldn't get a proper feel for this place if I was told what to see, where to go.

I moved on the thick, plush lawn toward the pines, the air brisk on my face, the sun shining in my eyes. The forest of pines stretched into shadows and I could not see, from my vantage, how far back it went.

I walked along the tree-line. Bird sounds surrounded me. A squirrel rushed from one tree to the next. The pines gave off a heady, cool scent. I followed the tree line as it wound about the complex and tapered off to a farmer's field some distance away.

Coming back uphill, green all around me, I realized I now faced the back of the chattel farm building. It was a huge complex. It housed single adult Omegas who serviced Alphas, as well as children and a school. I had nothing to criticize about the upkeep of this establishment. Maybe my dad had been cold, but he'd kept things running smoothly, and I did not see even one crack in the paint, not out front, and not here in the back.

I found a white cement path that took me closer to the building, and noted up ahead an area fenced off by chain link. That was when I saw the pool. It was behind that fence, glimmers of sapphire pulsating in daylight and surrounded by dozens of empty lounge chairs.

Slatted awnings jutted off the building's roof, creating shady spaces.

I came up to the fence and peered in. I couldn't see into the shadows. My eyes, from being in the sun, could not adjust. But I thought I heard someone give a little cough.

The pool area was in good repair, and the pool itself well maintained, though old-looking.

A gate stood partially open and I stepped through to get a better look.

Something moved in the shadows and I squinted. "Hello?"

I heard something that sounded like a whispered word. "Fuck."

"I'm sorry. I don't mean to intrude. The pool is lovely. What a peaceful space. I only wanted to see it closer, you understand."

"No. I don't understand," said the same voice, no longer whispering.

"Well, I'm with the group here touring the grounds. My name is Orion. I'm the one who's leaving a questionnaire for you all to fill out. Just to make sure--"

"I know who you are. The new owner. And you're checking out your investment, that's it."

The voice came out clipped and tough. I recognized it immediately. That tone belonged to the furious Omega from indoors.

"What's your name?" I asked.

"Why would you want to know that?"

"Curious, that's all. Plus, I was hoping to talk to a few of you individually, get your take on things."

"You can talk to the warden just fine. And the house-dads."

"Well, yes, but of course they'll tell me everything I want to hear. To please me."

A deeper shadow among the shadows moved. My eyes were slowly adjusting and I saw a form, the silhouette of a young man sitting in the lounge chair. A flicker of light caught on his vivid, dark hair.

"Everyone seems pretty content here. Well cared for. Healthy. Of that I'm glad." *But not him.* I waited for his response.

It took a few prolonged seconds before he said, "Do they? Good, then. A healthy, content Omega makes life easier for Alphas, doesn't rock the boat, and for that the world runs a little smoother, right?"

32

This one had a mouth on him for sure. I was certain the warden would not approve of how he spoke to me, but the warden wasn't here. It was just me and him. If I could get him to stop being so defensive, I might receive a little honesty from him.

"I am not sure that statement is true."

"No? Isn't that what every Omega is taught here? You're the owner now. Don't you know?"

"Pretending problems don't exist can cause them to grow, or repeat."

"Well, Mr. Boss Man, there are some problems too big to fix."

I took a step toward the edge of the pool.

The shadow jerked as if startled. "Stay where you are! Don't come closer!"

I stood very still, glancing at the silvery blue water before me. It was like a barrier between us. I wasn't anywhere near him.

There was a scent on the air like metal, almost like the taste of blood. Acrid sweat mixed with the pool's bleachy aroma. I blinked from the sting in my nose. From this distance, I scented him clear and pure. This Omega did not smell of fresh cut flowers like the usual ones I'd met. He was afraid.

"Not moving another inch," I said.

Silence.

I breathed in and out slowly. "Not all problems can be fixed, at least not easily. I know that."

I heard a sound like a snort.

"Maybe if you told me why you're unhappy I could--"

"Stop! Now you're going to ply me with some promise you can't keep?" A single laugh escaped the dimness, cutting the air.

"I can't try to make improvements here if I don't know what's wrong."

"You want to know what's wrong?"

Frowning, I nodded.

A hand moved in the slatted light shining through the awning at the edge of the shadows. It looked like a big moth taking off, then fluttering down for another landing. "What's wrong is everything, but you can't see that. And you most certainly can't fix it."

"Why not?"

"You're only one man. And you're an Alpha so there's no benefit to you."

"I don't understand." I wasn't sure where he was going with this.

"Why would you? It's been this way for so long you can't see what's right in front of you."

"What's right in front of me?"

"You think this is a safe space for Omegas? A wonderful resort where we get all we need?"

Wasn't it? I mean, yes, things might be able to be improved, but if I didn't get suggestions from Omegas, I wouldn't know what to do about that.

"Is it not safe here? Are you not safe?"

I heard another sort of cackle. Then he said, "No. It's not. And there's nothing to be done about it because this is a prison. You own a prison, Mr. Boss. How does that feel? All these Omegas are technically yours. Assets to be paid for, used and abused. There's a lot of money in that. Can you fix that problem, Mr. Boss? Can you make assurances that no Omega is ever touched by another Alpha except with total consent? Or promise that every Alpha in the Burn is in control?"

This was why I hated what my dad did for his living. This business. It was uncomfortable at best. But my usually cold dad also always used to say, "Where would all these Omegas go if we didn't house them and care for them? They need this and I provide it."

I accepted his words, though I didn't understand them. I'd never understood why young and unbonded Omegas were kept away, for the most part, from society. "To keep them safe" was the Alpha-invented excuse for the existence of the farms and even the private cloisters where I went to slake my fevers.

At the farms, I was taught, Alphas could also meet prospective Omega mates discreetly and safely. If Alphas and Omegas mingled freely in society, said my dad, there would be a lot more crime and the Omegas would suffer the brunt of it.

I didn't believe it because I didn't accept that we Alphas were all monsters.

But this boy, whose name I still didn't know, seemed to have a different perspective. And he was afraid. Somewhere, somehow, he'd met a monster or two, perhaps. Warden Chirl had said he'd suffered trauma.

It seemed impossible to think there would be any monsters here amid the sparkling water, the blue sky and sunshine, and the beautiful forest in the distance. Everything glimmered as if newly washed. The place seemed to be run efficiently. And Alpha customers were screened.

I'd never thought about consent because I'd been taught Omegas readily responded to Alphas in the Burn. There wasn't supposed to be a problem of them wanting the Alpha in return. In the end, it was only sex when one looked at it from the perspective of biology, of nature. Seemingly not a big deal. That's what all Alphas were taught.

"Keep telling yourself you help, that you care, that you keep Omegas safe. That our classes in cooking and sewing, homemaking and breeding, hair and makeup are all we need and what's best. Keep believing it, Mr. Boss-Man, Mr. Orion. You own our world now. You thought it would be easy, didn't you? You still think it. Go ahead. Take the profits and don't look any further."

"But that's why I'm here." His speech might have offended other Alphas, but not me. All I heard in his words was resentment and hatred. Maybe he had mental problems. I didn't know. But I would listen. He didn't sound irrational.

"No. It's not why you're here. You want to make sure you own something clean. Easy. If it's not to your liking, you can just sell it to another Alpha, wash your hands of it."

The truth slammed me. Shamed me. He spoke it as if he already knew about the conversation I'd had with Saben about wanting to sell.

I didn't want to be responsible for these people. I'd never thought about inheriting my dad's business, at least not until I was much, much older.

But now I was responsible. And I had a decision to make.

I took a step forward. "If we could talk a little more, maybe I could understand better."

"I said no closer!"

The shadow moved, dark on dark smoothly rising, a swath of white shirt and brilliant hair, the gleam of an eye catching the daylight rays for a moment, like an animal caught in headlights, only angry and caged.

He'd stood out in the front room, the most beautiful of them all with his darker veneer of disgust against the lineup of all the properly trained Omegas primped and preened to perfection to meet the Alpha tour group I'd brought with me.

Wild, hair in his eyes, this one sent my blood rushing.

"Best to stay away!" he yelled.

I heard a door snick open.

"Sell this place and don't think. Don't look back. You're one of the lucky. Born Alpha. Why would you even want to come here unless you were suffering the Burn? Or you wanted to make a claim?"

"I disagree. I really am interested in improving your lives here. Please, don't leave yet. I would like to talk more."

But I heard his footsteps click up a step. Saw the edge of his belt and the cuff of one sleeve in the darkness as he finally vanished, the door slamming closed behind him.

A blue jay flew up to the rooftop above where he'd been sitting. It let out a squawk and eyed me suspiciously.

I heard voices, then, and turned to see the group I'd come with appear around the bend of the complex.

"Ah," said Chirl. "I see you've found the pool."

"I have."

"Would you like a tour of the Children's Wing next?"

"That would be fine."

But I couldn't quite focus. The next hour was a blur.

Later, as we left, I handed the stacks of questionnaires to Chirl.

"I'll make sure these are handed out," he said.

"And one more question. Who was that Omega who spoke out in the front room when we first arrived?"

"What, sir?" he asked, his smile gone, his lips thinning.

"The one you told me had suffered a trauma. I simply wanted to know his name. Even the critiques of those who don't quite fit in here are valuable. I want to make sure I receive his questionnaire personally."

"His name is Holland, sir."

Holland. A beautiful name.

"He's not quite well, though. But he's being seen to and well cared for, I assure you. His answers may not be anything you want to hear."

"If I heard only what I wanted to hear, the place would already be perfect."

"I just meant, sir, that he might not make a lot of sense."

"Well, that will be for me to decide, right?" I didn't say anything about our little talk by the pool. How his words not only made some sense, but intrigued me.

Warden Chirl nodded, but a darkness had come over his eyes. I didn't like to see that the same as I didn't like to hear about prisons and selling Omegas and non-consent.

It had all fallen to me quicker than I could comprehend. Responsibility. Such a big word. But it crept over me and weighed on my shoulders.

Saben would be happy to hear I hadn't decided to sell Zilly's. Yet.

Chapter Five

Holland

Six foot three. Beautiful brown wavy hair. Bright, dark eyes. Muscles like chiseled marble that pulled and tugged at his sleeves, his shoulders, his thighs.

The new boss who now lorded over us all, who did the unthinkable and actually *toured* this place which no owner in my lifetime had done before, had the looks of a prince but more naiveté than an Omega sixth year schoolboy.

I'd smelled him on the breeze as he approached the pool. Earth. Fire. Rain. Alpha strut and Alpha privilege.

Danger.

My body, frozen to see him come close, closer, couldn't move and I watched from the shadows like some trapped animal hoping he'd wander off.

But he didn't. I had to make myself known to warn him away. But then, fuck all, he'd wanted to talk.

Typical behavior from what I knew about Alphas though I'd only ever met one. Taking what he wanted. No concern that I'd maybe come out there to be alone.

When I ran back inside the dorms, I still didn't feel safe.

Harly was there and he'd tried to talk to me.

"Isn't it great? Actual Alphas came for a tour. The owner himself! I've never seen one outside the mating hall."

"Yeah, wonderful to see our jailers in person."

"It wasn't like that. Why did you yell at them? I mean, that's maybe a little stupid, maybe brave, too, but mostly stupid."

"You calling me stupid?"

We had never fought before in all our years as friends, but at that moment we exchanged more not so nice words until his cheeks reddened. I wanted to slap them and redden them some more. Never until I'd turned eighteen and been attacked had I felt such violence in me.

Harly was pretty. Sweet. And he loved the sex he was allowed to have now. Completely opposite of me. He didn't deserve my ire.

"Just leave me alone!" I pulled away from his grasp and headed for my room.

I knew I'd hurt his feelings. He deserved better than me as a friend these days.

I couldn't be out there with the rest of them. I couldn't just join in the crowd, or just be me. I didn't know who "me" was anymore.

The Alpha had called himself Orion. His scent still stung my nose. His face, his hair and his whole body wouldn't leave my thoughts. Standing like he was in the sunlight, surrounded by green lawn and blue sky, like some kind of god just risen from the earth. I hated it. That image invaded my mind, taking over.

I threw myself onto my bed, hugging my pillow. My body shook.

He'd been big. He could have thrown me easily over his shoulder, taken me out into those pine woods and kept me there at his whim so I'd never be seen or heard from again. Instead, the arrogant prick had asked me questions like he fucking cared. It made me mad.

We told ourselves pretty little stories when we were young. Comfort stories about how great life could be for us. As Omegas, we would never have to worry about the stressful things like bills or complicated paperwork, taxes and politics and hard labor.

Our lovely heads need only focus on our mate, treating him well, keeping his house, raising his—hopefully Alpha—children. It was a joyful life we faced. But only if we were good and kept ourselves in shape so we would be chosen. So we could find a rich, caring Alpha bond-mate and live our happily ever after.

Such fairy tales. Stories to brighten the shadows and make our prison with its green lawns and lily pad ponds and warm beds less a cage and more a right.

How easily we believed how lucky we were to be naturally attuned to service such wonderful men during their poor, uncontrolled Alpha Burns. We helped them. We gave them peace and pleasure, and a reason to create such a lovely world so when their favor dictated we could partake in it as their beautiful and pampered other halves.

Or as I liked to think of it now, as their doting pets. Like dogs, we were trained to take a punch and come back, grudge-free, all doe-eyed and loyal.

Orion was only the second Alpha I'd ever met in my life. I hated him almost as much as I hated the man who'd raped and tortured me.

Why, then, as I fell to sleep that night, did I dream of him all the way until the next morning?

*

The next day, I avoided Harly and did not sit in the dining hall with our usual group. He kept giving me sidelong glances, which I pretended not to notice.

Everyone was talking about the questionnaire, which they'd all taken turns on the school computers filling out and emailing to the new Alpha owner.

They all seemed to feel special, being asked their opinions by an Alpha of such high regard.

Only I knew the truth. That this Alpha knew nothing about chattel farms, or Omegas as a rule. He didn't even know himself. He was big and pretty. So what? He had money. He held himself in a superior stance. We were all supposed to be impressed? All my friends were stupid and I didn't want to have anything to do with them anymore.

I'd seen that questionnaire. It had statements on it like:

What is your favorite hobby on the farm?

Do you enjoy school? If not, what could be handled better about school? If so, what is your favorite subject?

Is there a subject you would like to see taught that is not available on your school curriculum?

Is there an area of the farm that you can think of that might need improvement?

Are your teachers and house-dads fair to you?

Do you have needs that are not being met? If yes, use space below to give a brief description of such needs.

Do you feel confident you can meet your future Alpha mate from prospective clients of Zillys?

That last question was a doozy! A year ago, it might never have concerned me. But now?

And that question about needs being met: All the young kids talked about answering with stupid stuff like more cake for desserts, faster delivery of current vid games, or better hair products. I didn't read their emails. I only knew what they wrote because I heard them talking about it all day at every meal and in the commons rooms.

Orion. Orion. That's all I heard.

In the afternoon, Warden Chirl met me in the hall as I was making my way to the patio and pool again, my favorite place for quiet and relaxation. He'd been lax with me because of my injuries. Letting me get away with doing nothing but sleeping in, taking naps, watching movies. The Alpha doctors had said I needed lots of sleep to gain my normal, healthy strength.

"Holland." He reached out as if to touch my shoulder but stopped an inch away from the cloth of my shirt.

"Yes, sir." I kept my voice low.

"You didn't fill out a questionnaire."

"No, sir."

"May I ask why? They are confidential. You can say whatever you wish. Orion will be discreet."

"I just didn't do it." My eyes focused on a small spot of floor past Chirl's left side about six feet away. The floor wax had worn away and it wasn't as shiny as the rest. The smear looked like a devil face, complete with horns and pointy ears.

"Well, please do. Every voice counts. This is a good thing. Omegas don't always get a voice in Alpha affairs, you know."

"I don't want to answer those questions, sir."

"Why ever not?"

I scratched at the back of my head, digging my fingernails in hard until I felt pain. "They're stupid."

"What? Well." He paused.

"If every opinion counts, sir, then that's my opinion."

"There is a place at the end of the document where you can write your thoughts, anything not covered in the list. Perhaps you can make suggestions of better questions to ask."

Yeah, there had been a space at the end. It was there for anyone who felt intensely verbose and wanted to write an essay about their experiences here.

A waste of time, I thought.

"Do you think you could at least put a comment in? Anything at all, even if it's negative. It helps give perspective. This is an important thing that is happening here."

"I don't know why you would say that, sir. The new Alpha owner is young. He just doesn't know any better yet how things work."

"Hmm." Chirl put his hand to his mouth as if thinking.

I looked up from the devil in the floor to his face. He wasn't mad. He had the kind of patience with the worn, slightly frazzled edges that all unbonded Omegas wore on their faces. Heavy lines, sagging muscles. The word to describe that was forlorn.

"You're very young to have such observations. I understand you've been through a nightmare. But the world

42

is changing, not like it was when I was your age. We had even less rights, then. It will be the younger Alphas like Orion who will change it. I believe that."

The muscles in my face hardened; my eyebrows narrowed. It seemed as though I was looking at the warden through a dark tunnel and he stood in the small light at the end but it didn't matter because he was too far off. The darkness around me had hands, teeth, claws. It held me fast and hard, with rippling strength that drew blood.

"Take a look at the questions again." Chirl kept his voice level, gentle.

I did not hide my heavy sigh. "Yes, sir."

"That's all I ask."

He turned away, then, letting me do as I pleased, requiring nothing of me. How long that would last, I didn't know. But I appreciated his patience if nothing else here on the farm.

All day and into the next, I couldn't bring myself to take a second look at Orion's meaningless questionnaire. It was pointless, and the questions vapid at best.

Why should I give Orion anything? Just because he had spoken soft like the winds above the pines beyond the acres of lawn, and stopped moving toward me when I told him to stop, and just because he projected a fiery, smoky scent that still would not leave the back of my throat, and puffed his smooth, tanned cheeks out when he sort of smiled at me. Just because of all that didn't mean I owed him.

He hadn't dragged me away to the pine forest. He was supposed to get credit for that?

I sat by the glimmering pool all afternoon. No one came out to the patio. Autumn had passed and now we were into early winter. Though the weather had been mild for the past week, it was still too late in the year and too cold to swim.

Before bed, I went to one of the computer rooms in the school and brought up the questions one more time.

Damn Chirl!

I didn't re-read the form, but quickly scrolled to the bottom where the space was for a short essay.

I began to type.

Classes in pre-med, law, higher science and mathematics are missing here at Zilly's.

Where are all the Omega doctors, lawyers, politicians and astronauts in your world?

Answer: Non-existent because we have no access to higher learning not even if we're raised by loving parents in higher homes. It just isn't done... teaching Omegas these things might worry their pretty heads.

Of course we have no rights, so cannot hold bank accounts, let alone any real jobs short of day to day organization on Omega farms, cooking and cleaning and teaching and caring for the young. Oh, and maybe some secretarial work on the side.

But that's not something you can fix.

You want to fix the problems with Zilly's. Right? Like roof leaks and paint chipping away and whether or not our computer system runs fast enough in the classrooms.

Do the stoves work so we can eat? Are we wearing clothes that actually fit? Are we sufficiently entertained with games, books, movies? Are our spaces well-lit and clean?

Pour some money into this place and we'll all get fat on cake every day with plastered grins on our faces from the heaving orgasms we get from big, buff Alphas paying top dollar to visit our mating halls.

We're all just fine here.

Unless you can alter the whole fucking world and its deranged belief systems and power-mad, sex-starved leaders...

Leave us alone!

I didn't re-read what I wrote. I clicked send so hard I thought I'd broken the mouse.

Afterward, I sent a brief email to Chirl telling him I had, indeed, sent in my questionnaire.

Like the good little Omega I was supposed to be.

One of the boys I didn't know very well from the dorms furthest from my own, came through the dining hall with a stacks of mail.

Most of the time, none of us new adults got anything. Sometimes, if Alphas were trying to court an Omega, they sent more than texts or emails, stuff like cards, little gifts or flowers. To be claimed by an Alpha who wanted to attempt the mate-bond was the goal. The dream. Most of us pined away our whole lives waiting for that to happen.

The percentage of Omegas here at Zilly's who found bondmates was high. There weren't many who stayed on past the age of thirty. Those who did stay often entered into service here. Warden, therapist, house-dad, to name a few of the spaces that were filled by older Omegas.

The boy with the mail passed by me where I sat alone finishing my lunch of baked chicken and a green salad.

"Holland," he said casually, and a white envelope fluttered to the tabletop and settled next to my right hand.

"What?" I snarled. It wasn't that I meant to be impolite to him, but in fact he had startled me.

The boy continued on as if he didn't hear my question.

Frowning, I picked up the envelope. In curly, neat handwriting was my name printed right in the center. *Holland.* No stamp. No return address. Nothing to indicate where the mail had originated.

I lifted the edge to my nose to see if it held any scent, only to realize how paranoid that seemed. I breathed in clean paper scent, a bit woodsy, nothing more.

Slowly, I opened the flap and pulled out a folded letter.

When I opened it, I saw it was handwritten in the same script my name had been scrawled, not typed and printed out as most letters would be. But written with a pen. And not so little flourish.

The ink was dark blue.

The first line below the date read, again: *Holland.*

Quickly, I glanced at the bottom of the letter.

The signature, larger than the rest with wider drawn letters and big O's, read *Orion*.

A throb began in my temples. Something light and airy seemed to bubble up in my chest. A tickling sensation that was almost pain but not quite.

Why would the new owner be writing to me? The Alpha who had dragged me off in my dreams was someone I'd hoped to forget. But I couldn't forget he was too young to know what he owned in Zilly's, and that thought he was doing Omegas a favor by asking them questions pertaining to their needs.

I wanted to laugh out loud. I wanted to tear the paper in my hand into little bits and scatter them like confetti about the room. But my eyes drew toward the body of the letter and couldn't help but begin to read.

Holland:

Your essay caught my eye, and then I remembered you. From the front room where we were introduced to the crowd. And from the pool area. I remember your boldness. Your discontent.

Your warden had given me your name.

How could I forget such a spirited man? Someone who dared to tell me the truth?

I would like to open a discourse with you about Zilly's and the improvements I intend to make. If you have the time.

I sensed discomfort upon our first meeting, so I understand if you would not wish to meet face to face for further discussion.

Email will be fine. My address is:

xxxxx.com

Should you decide you might wish to meet, I can send a car around.

I can guarantee your safety at any meeting with me. If you do not feel secure, I will allow you to bring a friend to join our discourse.

I confess I sent this letter the old-fashioned way to get your attention. I was afraid if I sent a simple email, it would go unread. Or you would not take it seriously that you have been heard.

Thank you for your time.

Your friend in hopes of making a darker world a bit brighter,

Orion.

I held the letter tight in my fist and gave a low laugh that startled the boys on the other side of the table. They looked up, curious, but said nothing.

My laugh got creakier, and maybe even scary. I didn't care.

This was the most ridiculous letter ever.

"Got an Alpha on the hook?" one of them said.

I had grown up with these guys, all of us attending some of the same classes. The one who spoke was Zeke, and he looked inordinately pleased with his question.

"Not likely," I said.

"Well, then, are you gonna tell us?"

One table over, Harly turned to look at me. We hadn't spoken in a couple days and I felt badly about that. I met his eyes, then looked away.

"None of your business," I said, addressing Zeke.

Zeke and his friends rolled their eyes at me, and continued eating their lunch.

Right after lunch, I went back to my room and hid the letter under my pillow. I was going to toss it, but I worried that someone might find it in the trash. It was stupid, really. I didn't want anyone to know about the letter, or that it had come from Orion. I wasn't sure why I cared. In some weird way, it embarrassed me. Orion had written so formally. He had treated my off-hand, smart-ass comments with respect.

Why would he do that?

Obviously, my essay had been pure sarcasm, nothing more. I'd certainly disrespected his actions, yet he came back for more. I didn't understand it at all.

Glancing at the clock on my bed stand, I saw I had five minutes before my therapist appointment.

I snorted at the empty room, wondering what Sen would want to discuss today. My PTSD? My future here at the farm? My dreams of ever finding a bondmate dashed and broken like a pretty glass figurine now in a million pieces all over the floor?

The worst would be if he asked about my dreams. I always lied anyway about everything these days, so of course I wouldn't say my nightmares of the attack had been replaced with dreams of a big, dumb, rich Alpha who stood before a sizzling blue swimming pool and kept asking me inane questions about what it was like living on the farm. Oh and were my needs being met?

Sometimes I woke laughing, though I didn't find it funny at all.

But it certainly made my sleep easier, even if my moods had not really improved.

I combed my hair and brushed my teeth, then moved out into the hall and headed for Sen's office.

When I pushed the door open, Sen was waiting for me, standing by the window and looking out over the lush lawn that sloped at the back of the farm. He had a funny look on his face as he turned to greet me. Like his eyes held all the beauty of this place but his mind was trapped.

Unmated, unbonded, did he see the prison as I did? Had he always seen it?

When he heard my footfalls, he turned and smiled his greeting a little too quickly for me to believe he was at all happy to see me.

"Holland, come in. Welcome." He went to his desk and, still standing, tapped a few keys on his computer keyboard.

I stepped inside the room and let the door shut behind me.

"Shall we get started?" His voice punched the air, almost forcefully bright.

"Do I have a choice?"

Chapter Six

Orion

The paper sat on my dad's desk.

It was the one partially filled out questionnaire from Zilly's that had thrown me. I couldn't forget it. I couldn't stop reading it over and over again.

I'd printed it out so I could hold it as I read it for the tenth time.

The damaged Omega who'd spoken out in the crowd, and who'd later yelled at me to stay away from him when I'd encountered him at the pool area had written it.

Holland.

I'd asked his name before I left the tour. It matched the one on the paper.

When I'd asked Warden Chirl if Holland had always been an upstart, his face, just for a second, tightened as if he felt pain. He pressed his lips together in a line before replying, as if it was a matter-of-fact for him. "His first time with an Alpha was not good. He was attacked. It's been hard for him."

"Attacked? Aren't your clients screened?"

"To the best of our abilities, yes."

When I had pressed Chirl for more details, he had replied only, "He's getting the best help, medical treatment and therapy."

I remembered standing again in the front hall, looking around at the Omegas who again gathered to see me off. Holland had not been among them.

Their faces were mostly young. The older ones left behind were still waiting to be claimed or had given up the mating hall for whatever reasons they might have, and stayed on to serve the farm in other capacities.

Still, to my mind, all were beautiful, flushed and waiting for opportunity, for a dream to come to them in the form of a bondmate, for the world to open up and give them a chance.

In a flash I had seen how vulnerable they were even in the clean and warm environment of Zilly's, circled by a pine forest, surrounded by rolling green lawns.

Their eyes had watched me, wide and bright, a little unsure but still hopeful.

A realization spread through me, like being drenched in cold water.

It was no matter that they might be pampered, healthy, and ready to meet Alphas. I saw them for what they were to the Alpha population. Prey. Caged. Waiting for the predator to pet them, feed them, notice them.

I decided to write a personal letter to Holland. I felt it was mandatory so he would know without a doubt his words had been heard.

He was correct in every point he made. I could not fix the world. I could only help those who happened to cross my path.

Answering him required me to ignore his last sentence: *Leave us alone!*

But I wanted him to know I had read his words. I felt as the new owner of Zilly's, I owed him that much. There was a personal aspect to it, too, however. I could not get his furious face out of my thoughts.

I never expected a reply.

Holland did not send a letter. Instead, two days later, I received an email.

Orion:

I find it strange that you sent me a real letter. Is that even done anymore?

I can only assume the discourse you want with me is perhaps more hands on?

I am not comfortable meeting Alphas face to face, even ones who "send a car," if I have a choice.

If it makes your day, then by all means, email away with all your thoughts about making this dark world a brighter place. It will entertain me, at least, and at best I will get a nice laugh out of it.

You might think shipping to the farm better hair products, silk robes, cake and more flashy toys for the younger ones is helping. That if you can make us feel better about ourselves you're chasing away the shadows. Well, the sun can shine all it wants but it doesn't change the fact that surrounding it is infinite void, and the stars are so far apart they can't even touch. Did you know the light of the closest star takes 4.37 years to reach us?

You cannot change the laws of physics. You alone cannot change the law of our world.

It amuses me you want to even try. However, it does not surprise me. Only Alpha arrogance could be so blind.

Holland

*

The email came just after I'd looked up Holland's files. As owner, I had access to them all. I could read all his grades from every year of classes since he was five years old. I could see every note his therapist had made in the weeks since the attack upon him. All his private medical files were open to me.

As owner of Zilly's, Holland had no privacy from me. I had the right to look at every word that had been filed on him, every record, every report and every photo and vid that had ever been made.

Sure it was legal for me to have all this, but I couldn't stop picturing his face scrunched up in fury, and I felt like a creep looking it all over. Like I was watching him when he didn't know I was looking.

Sure, Alphas could be creeps but I didn't want to be one of them.

However, I could not look away from his most recent medical report. I went cold inside as I read how he had been so brutally raped and tortured. He'd had a broken wrist, broken knuckles, fractured ribs and a badly sprained ankle. He'd been torn in the most private of places. He'd been bruised badly all over his body and a photo of his face inserted with the online file showed him so swollen and purple he was unrecognizable.

I had to sit with my eyes closed for a moment to calm myself before I went to the Alpha vetting service for Zilly's and researched it.

The service they used had a website and a form to fill out. I took one look at the form and realized it wasn't good enough. It did not force Alphas to give enough sources for staff background checks. It wasn't required and of course they made minimal effort to check Alpha status before giving the green light for an Alpha to use Zilly's Omega services.

I sent emails to my staff to ask the vetting company to come up with a more detailed form for background checks, or fire the service and find a better one. I insisted in depth records on Alphas re-using Zilly's services be kept and updated every six months.

They'd hate me for the extra work but I didn't care. I wasn't my dad and I wasn't going to blindly follow in his footsteps. If I kept Zilly's, I was going to make sure the higher class establishment that Zilly's was ran as well as possible. It made plenty of profit. There was no excuse for short-cuts.

Accidents like what happened to Holland should never happen. I knew it was impossible to one hundred percent prevent that sort of thing—determined Alphas could get away with a lot and never be labeled or punished—but anything I could do to make my Omegas safer, I would do.

My Omegas?

Why was I even thinking that way?

Of course, I owned the farm. A chattel farm. *Chattel* really was an unfortunate word used commonly in society that made it seem as if they were nothing more than stock, like farm animals.

Technically, legally, I did own them.

Ethically, it was a horror for me to even think it.

Finally, I wrote back to Holland.

Chapter Seven

Holland

I pulled up Orion's second email on a new tablet I'd
received when a shipment of tablets, laptops and reader units
arrived several nights after Holland's tour.

We'd all had reading tablets before, but none with the
ability to connect to wifi. To go online, we had to use the
classroom computers.

Orion changed all that for us in a heartbeat.

I hadn't asked for this. But someone among us must
have.

Usually, requests at Zilly's for updated equipment or
repairs or supplies that were different from the norm took
weeks to be processed with tons of paperwork. Often those
requests were denied. Orion was new. I was sure he would
soon lose interest trying to impress us.

My opinion was no Alpha would allow his life to
become tangled up in the interests of mere Omegas, none of
whom were his bondmates or regulars who serviced him.

His email to me, when it came, was a surprise. But I
wasn't going to allow myself to believe in his visions. They
weren't real. He'd only disappoint everyone in the end.

Still, I read his words.

Twice.

Holland:

*I understand your fears and appreciate that you offer any
discourse, email or otherwise.*

Thank you.

I don't know if I can convince you to believe me or not, but I do not blindly agree with all Alpha laws.

It is only recently that I inherited Zilly's. I had no idea what to expect. I do not use chattel farms myself, so touring Zilly's the day we met was my first time setting foot on one.

I had wanted to sell Zilly's right away, but my lawyer convinced me to look first before I made any decision.

Now I am leaning toward deciding to keep the farm.

Why the change of mind?

Maybe you have already guessed.

Your outburst. My meeting with you.

You made an impact whether it was your intention or not. If I have the power to make life better for a few Omegas, why turn away from that?

I feel I must be honest. I had no altruism in my heart when I first entered the doors of Zilly's.

Now, however, I feel an urge to do better. I can only start with what I have. I have the farm.

I know from your warden you suffered trauma. That is unconscionable to me. If I can make sure that what happened to you never happens to another Omega—at least on my property—I will do that.

Your input is valuable. You have a unique point of view I do not have.

I know my questions seem very general for now. But I have to start somewhere.

What changes would you like to see me make?

Orion

I sat motionless for a few moments staring out the window, the tablet in my lap.

Around me, my dorm-mates who hadn't been assigned servicing duties for the day watched TV, played video games, or sat around talking and eating snacks. The sound level was not high, but I heard every word, every clothing rustle, every footstep. They were too loud, all of them.

I had a fury in me that made me want to stand up and yell at them all to shut up. I wanted to hit something. I wanted to scream.

I got up and left the room, slamming the door behind me. The only place that offered peace and quiet was the patio that faced the pool.

I headed there at a fast pace, chin down, not wanting to meet the eyes of anyone I might encounter along the way.

The chlorine scent mixed with the fresh cut lawn beyond the fence. It instantly settled me. The cold, pale blues of the pool water washed through my mind. My breathing slowed.

Locating my favorite lounge chair, I sat in the slatted shadows and stared through the chain link fence toward the pine forest at the edge of the farm.

The day was cool but I liked it. My skin prickled and the air seeped into me until I felt very little, which was what I preferred.

I lifted my tablet, hit reply to Orion's email, and began to type.

By the end my hands were shaking. From the cold, I told myself. From the cold.

Orion:

Your bleeding heart is on overtime, I see.

It doesn't really impress me. Your pity. Your change of mind about selling the farm.

Oh, did you mean for it to impress me?

Did you peek at my records?

I'm sure you did.

If so, then you well understand that my life is over. I have no freedom to seek my dreams. If I refuse to serve in the mating hall, I have no other recourse but to become a servant to Omegas here who are healthy and willing to serve Alphas.

My lack of excitement over that isn't anything to do with this place being clean, functional, or meeting the essential needs of

56

Omegas who live here. It's all just fine. How would you really improve on that beyond sending us better food or toys?

The problems with the farm are intrinsic to the nature of an Omega's rights, or lack thereof.

These changes you make affect nothing.

For me, the problems I have are mine, and are personal. They are about the fact that I will never find a bondmate, never have a family, whether I wanted one or not, because I have no freedom to seek anything in any other way but servicing Alphas and waiting for one to claim me.

There is no such thing as a free Omega. Period. End of argument.

What can you do about that?

How can you change that?

These are rhetorical questions that have no answers. I know that.

If I don't bend over, my life is useless in an Alpha ruled world. I have no place. Of course a place will be made for me here on the farm.

But that was never my dream when I was young. To stay here forever? To never know the outside?

Not my choice.

Nothing can be done.

Maybe this discourse is over now. That will be fine. A relief, actually.

Holland

I sent the email without allowing myself second thoughts. I didn't check for spelling errors. I didn't care. I wanted it out there, off my chest. It was too much weight for me to hold onto.

Orion himself was too much weight. An Alpha who pretended to care. I couldn't allow myself to comprehend that right now.

I could tell by his email that he had looked at my private records. He knew all that had happened to me. He had the right to know. But it made my mind spin.

Every time he wrote to me, he would be thinking of me as the boy who'd been raped. The scarred boy. The ruined boy. How could he see me in any other light?

No one could. Even Sen couldn't comprehend it. I was used and thrown away like garbage. I wasn't trying to feel sorry for myself. But the facts were the facts. People got hurt, sure, and accidents happened. But this was no accident. I was flung into this situation by a system that took away all control from me.

I might have made the best of my lack of choices if I hadn't been so brutally awakened to the horror of it all. I might have gone on in a stupor like the others, happy to be given steak and extra dessert on Sundays, happy to get my rocks off with burly Alphas whose Burns gave off a spiced scent that made me slick and willing to fuck.

But that page had turned. My new life's page was a misprint, a page of gray and black swirls where the language had smeared.

"It will get better," Sen had said to me all too often. "Give it time."

But the people who knew me would always look at me differently.

Orion could not know that the humiliation was even worse with him because he was Alpha, and because he held so much power over Zilly's, over all the Omegas housed here. Over me.

I blinked hard but my eyes remained dry. I was stone. I had nothing to give anyone.

Dashing that email off to Orion felt good. As if I'd finished something too overwhelming to even begin.

I set my tablet in my lap, closed my eyes, and let the cool air fill me up with nothing.

Chapter Eight

Orion

Tight mouth. Fury in the eyes. Posture stiff, almost pained.

I remembered nothing from the tour but Holland. Every line of his face, the way his arms folded tense across his chest, how his mouth curved up and down at almost the same time like a grimace to the world and a flat out rejection of life itself.

That was not how Holland looked in the older vids and photos I now paged through on the computer from his files.

In one vid, he was sweet and smiling as he accepted his high school diploma one month before his attack, walking on a stage with a group his own age. Holland was first in line because he'd ranked highest in his class. His grades had been impeccable, but the subjects disappointed me. I had never realized they were so limited for Omegas. Home economics. Cooking. Sewing. Health and fitness. Health and sexuality. Reading. And there had been art where he'd learned how to make paper mache hats and masks. And he'd gotten A's in diapering baby dolls and learning how to keep house.

The brightest. The prettiest. That was how others described Holland.

I looked into his files that applied to the mating hall.

Omegas were not allowed to know about or discuss the money they made at Zilly's. But I had access to all.

He'd been put up for top dollar, one of the highest amounts ever, which also took into account his virginity. And the first man to ask for him and pay that fortune had been the one to ruin him.

It was wrong.

The Alpha in question was named Bosk and he had gone to jail for a couple weeks. He had supposedly been diagnosed with a treatable type of schizophrenia. He'd been given prescriptions, labeled dangerous, then allowed his freedom. It was a slap on the wrist and an insult to Holland.

If Bosk stood in front of me this very moment, I cannot say I wouldn't try to kill him.

An urge in me to make sure Holland was safe surged through me like a strange, warm tide, settling just below my breastbone. It almost hurt.

But what could I do? He wouldn't see me. He was trapped in his closed-in life at the farm and I had no power I could foresee to change that circumstance.

I sat down and composed several emails to him before settling on a final draft. I was not sure he would ever answer, but it seemed right that I still had to try to keep in contact with him, keep him talking.

Holland:

You ask truly hard questions, ones that I cannot give solace on, except maybe philosophically.

You seem to operate under the notion that Alphas and Omegas cannot be friends. You are not the only one. Most Alphas believe this. But I think it is a false belief.

We are people first and foremost. We can connect on levels other than our societal labels.

I know I hold all the cards here. I own Zilly's. I own all within its walls, including you. That means I have the power to do whatever I want.

I could take you away from Zilly's.
I could show you the world you said you will never see.
I could do that as a friend.
But we are not yet friends. Could we be?

Orion

When I hit *send*, I shut my eyes as if I'd done a bad thing.

Would Holland think I was propositioning him? I wasn't. It was more an urge to do the right thing. Help him. Save him. Why not the others? I couldn't say, except, again, I will admit he stood out to me. He challenged roles: mine, his. He made me feel a wind in my solar plexus.

I didn't know him. I'd only seen him twice, briefly, that one day. We'd exchanged only a few tense emails.

What was the matter with me?

I couldn't save every Omega. But Holland stood in my mind like a warrior who'd broken into my private rooms and refused to leave.

I couldn't stop thinking about him.

*

The sun set in bright pink and orange stripes out my office window. Sometimes the twilight made me feel like I was drowning. When I was a kid, I remember a restlessness overcoming me at twilight, as if I were being touched by a dozen ghosts.

Because I'd decided to keep Zilly's, I now had a part time job. I spent the afternoon online approving orders, reading emails and messages pertaining to Zilly's. I was learning the ropes.

Most of the work to maintain the farm took care of itself, but as the owner I had to approve things. I had to okay daily reports and financial documents.

There was a lot to learn.

As I got up to stretch, my email dinged. Again.

I almost walked away, thinking I'd get some dinner and return to it all in the morning, but I glanced down.

Holland's address winked at me.

I sat down to read.

Orion

I cannot believe you would say those things. Offer me the world, like dangling a carrot in front of a horse's face with a plan to take it away.
And you did it so poorly, as if it means nothing.
How dare you?
We are not friends.
I would never trust you even if you said we were.
Where does that leave us?

Holland

I let my breath out fast.
"Wow," I said to my empty office.
To be perfectly honest, did I expect him to receive my thoughts with open arms? Did I ever think he'd allow me to take him away from the farm? I was a stranger. I was no one to him.
Of course he would be incapable of trust. He was tormented. He had to hate all Alphas.
At the same time, I couldn't deny my disappointment, as well as the thought that any of the Omegas in his age group would probably have jumped at the chance to go away with me with the guarantee of protection and no strings.
Holland had every reason to be bitter and wary.
And I was a stupid fool.
I wrote back a short response.

Holland:

I thought you might say that.
I am sorry you cannot believe that my intentions are good, and that I would guarantee your safety.
I still have need of an assistant to help me see to the smooth running of the farm.

If you can continue to write to me about how to improve all conditions at Zilly's, I will listen. I will respond.

Orion

I clicked *send* again, turned away from my computer and called a friend to meet me for dinner.

When I came home, I looked up at the sky and its sweeping horizons of stars never ending. And the closest star was 4.37 light years away.

I felt that wind in my chest.

I saw Holland's tense face. His streaming hair. I could not get him out of my mind.

When I passed by my office on my way to bed, I saw the computer flashing a message. With only the hall light shining into the room, I approached the computer. Holland's email address blinked at me, too bright in the semi-darkness.

I opened it and read it while standing in the stripe of light cast by my computer screen.

Orion:

I don't care what you do.

But my friends might have requests. More requests than simple tablets with online access. Will you listen to them? Any of them?

I don't want to play middleman. But I have overheard conversations. Unlike me, they are excited about Zilly's new owner. About you. They would love to make wish lists. Would that be possible for them?

Holland

"Unlike me, they are excited..." I read aloud.

The room held no response.

Okay, so he hated me. That was not news. Still, I frowned.

It was late but not too late. I figured he probably would not reply.

I sat down, composed, and sent.

Holland:

I will look at wish lists.
I can even set you up in a paid position to be the advocate for your Omega friends. The warden has too many responsibilities to be that for all of you.
I would keep your salary in trust for you, and you could spend it as you please.
This is an honest offer.

Orion

I sat with my hands folded on my stomach, watching the still screen. I waited five minutes.

A reply came in.

"That was fast," I said to the screen.

Orion:

Would I get my own office?

Holland

I laughed out loud and began to type.

Holland:

Overlooking the lily pond if you want.

Orion

Only two minutes passed this time.

Orion:

I want it overlooking the swimming pool.

Holland

We were having a real conversation. My heart sped up.

Holland:

An office overlooking the swimming pool. Done.

Orion

One minute passed.

Orion:

How soon can it be set up?

Holland

I typed fast, unable to keep the smile from my face.

Holland:

Is tomorrow soon enough?

Orion

Less than a minute later:

Orion:

I suppose that will have to do.

Holland

My laugh filled up the empty, dusky room my office. I had never turned on a proper light, but it was peaceful like this with just the glow of the computer screen and the amber hall light pinpointing this new reality I had entered.

Holland.

I could never tell him this moment made me feel closer to an Omega than I'd ever been, or he'd keep himself away from me. Forever.

But if I were to be completely truthful, he was everything I had ever wanted in an Omega.

Chapter Nine

Holland

The stained glass dragonfly lamp bathed the room in a low pink glow.

It was my favorite item in the office. I didn't ask for it. When the room was set up for me this morning, and a new desk, desk chair and couch brought in, as well as a computer with a huge monitor, the lamp also showed up. The lamp made the room less sterile, more mine, even though I didn't think of anything in it as completely *mine* yet.

Orion made good on his promise and got me a room for my office along the hall usually reserved for teachers. The window faced the pool patio.

I wondered who had been moved out of here to accommodate me. I didn't usually come into this area unless I had a meeting with a specific teacher, and that had happened only when I was younger, and rarely.

I had already opened the window to the fresh air and chlorine scent that calmed me.

I sat in my chair and stared out at the rippling blue water and the chain link fence beyond which the rolling lawn seemed to stretch without end. I did not turn on the computer yet. I tried to bask in this new space, this strange job I'd gotten all because I'd written a condescending email to the new Alpha owner of Zilly's.

I should have felt great, light as air. Instead, there was a sort of thickness in me, like a wind full of thunder, or what a jungle might feel like, hot and damp, pressing into eyes and skin and mouth.

What had I done? What had I really gotten myself into here?

I did nothing for two hours.

Sen and Chirl stopped by, each on his own, to see how I was doing and if I needed anything.

They were ever vigilant in looking out for me. Both men really did care about me. Chirl had known me my whole life. Sen knew me better now than most. But in their eyes I saw my reflection in the narrowing of the brows and the extra sheen of moisture in their gazes. They saw a victim, a boy to be pitied. The rape and torture was the visage I wore in their gazes and I could never escape that.

Maybe they were right to see me that way.

My wrist still ached late at night, as well as my ankle, though everything had healed well. All the bruises were gone from the outside,

Inside, however, told another story.

It was late in the day when I finally turned on the computer.

Already I was getting tons of emails from my brothers here, as well as the workers, those who taught, cooked, cleaned, babysat, and served us Omega to Omega.

I separated the wish lists into categories: Immediate Needs, Long-term Needs, and Luxuries. I figured I'd add subcategories as I went.

It was tedious to go over all the lists, but I lost myself in the work and before I knew it, a knock came at my door and I realized it was dark out.

I got up and opened it.

Harly stood in the hall. "They sent me to tell you you're missing dinner."

"I didn't realize the time."

We stared at each other. We hadn't really spoken since I'd yelled at him.

He peered around my shoulder. "It's nice," he said. "A whole office all your own and you're not even nineteen yet."

"I suppose."

"The new owner. Orion. He did this."

"Yeah, well, go figure. I sent him a nasty email and this is the result. You should try it."

Harly's face changed, and I saw that look. The pity. The sorry-for-me gaze I hated. I started to have second thoughts about this job. Did Harly see this as a pity-office? Did they all?

"I'll be there in a minute," I said gruffly, and turned away. I heard his footsteps recede down the hall.

*

Over the next weeks, Orion got a lot of things accomplished on the farm based on wish lists I organized. We had roof repairs done. The kitchen ovens which were very old were all replaced. The school rooms were newly painted. And out on the yard by the Children's Wing, they all got a new playground. He also granted a wish we all thought would never happen unless or until we met our true bondmates: He bought all the twelve-and-olders their own pairs of jeans.

Blue jeans ruled. Seeing actors on TV wearing them, or models in magazines, created a passion for them. Everyone wanted them. Alphas bought them for their Omega mates on the outside, and we saw evidence of it in the media. The Omegas on TV looked good. We wanted to be just like they were, happy, mated, safe and cared for, and wearing jeans.

Boxes of brand new blue jeans in all sizes arrived at the farm.

We were allowed to wear them on weekends unless we were summoned to the mating hall. Then it was back to the uniform: black slacks, white shirt.

I saw a glimmer of change in the attitudes of others on the farm after Orion became the new owner.

Growing up here, we knew nothing else. We had perfectly fine childhoods raised in groups by kind, unbonded Omegas who loved children. We were loved in that all our needs were met. We formed sibling relationships and friendships in our groups. Our Omega nannies tucked us into our beds at night.

Until we became teenagers, we hadn't realized the limitations of our world yet.

As we got older and understood what being Omega meant in the greater sense, some embraced it. But some of us suffered more than others. Depression made its dark rounds. Some got counseling. Some got drugs.

None of that happened to me. I'd been good. Obedient. Ready for my first mating. I was taught I would respond to the Alpha Burn with a chemical response of my own that would make me ready and want sex. I would feel great pleasure, and I looked forward to it.

But the darkness of the world, and the limited outlooks for those who were born Omegas, crashed down on me all at once

Reality changed for me. Or maybe it had always been the same reality but I had not looked at it face on. I had not fully comprehended how small my world really was, and how unsafe even on the farm.

But since Orion came, more Omegas smiled often. An electricity filled the air. People were more energetic. Upbeat.

I didn't dare have any hopes for myself beyond the farm, but I did enjoy wearing my new pair of jeans.

Orion wanted reports on everything. I kept myself cool and distant, and sent him the bare facts. Yes, the kids liked the new playground. Yes, everyone was excited about getting jeans for the first time ever.

He always wrote me in a polite and positive way about my terse reports. He never criticized.

Holland:

I am very happy to do what I can to make life at the farm better.

I'm gratified to hear you all enjoyed the gift of blue jeans. I had not realized jeans might be such a coveted item.

And the new playground is a hit? Good!

Repairs to the roof are finished and I will get a crew to start on replacing the old and cracked windows in the south wing.

I was wondering if, after all this success, you might like to celebrate.

70

I could send a car to pick you up and we could go out to dinner.

Again, I would like to state I can guarantee your safety. You would have no worries and a good meal. No strings.

Please say yes.

Orion

It was not unheard of for Omegas to go out on dates with Alphas outside their Burns. We would be given permission to sign out temporarily and spend time getting to know a man who might later make a legal claim for us. It was the goal of all, Omegas and Alphas alike.

But half the time, things didn't go that way. If an Alpha took a liking to an Omega and wanted him, he simply made a legal claim. He didn't have to work for it.

The claimed Omega had no freedom to object to this sort of arrangement. But most of them wanted to go. Most wanted off the farm, and to create a mate-bond and start a family.

The claim lasted for one year. If, in that time, no mate-bond was formed, or for whatever reason the Alpha was not satisfied with his claim, the Omega would be returned to the farm to be claimed again.

I looked at Orion's email, my insides beginning to tremble. What if he wanted to make a claim? I would not have the power to say no.

It would be better not to meet again. I could say no to the dinner. I still had that power. And I needed to keep what little power I had so no Alpha ever touched me again.

Orion:

A lot is being accomplished on the farm. Yes, it is very gratifying.

No, I will not have dinner with you. I prefer to stay here on the farm and work with you through more long-distance communication.

I do not need to celebrate every little matter that is fixed on the farm. It is good work, but it needed to be done anyway. It's not a victory, just the right thing to do.

If you disagree, I have more arguments I can put to you.

Holland

*

So much was wrong with me that I continued to send Orion rude emails at least once a day. He might not deserve it, but I couldn't curb my behavior.

In fact, my ruder emails got faster replies. They never seemed to faze him.

Over the next few weeks, Orion asked me out to dinner two more times, always making sure to guarantee my safety.

In my last response to him, I wrote one word. "No!"

Until the day came Warden Chirl called me into his office again.

I thought he was calling me to a meeting about Orion. Maybe Orion complained about my behavior. Although that seemed unlikely. If Orion had problems with me, he didn't seem the type not to face me with them.

Chirl stood up as I entered his office, his posture tall and tight, his chin up. He did not look at me as he motioned with one hand for me to take a seat across from him.

I watched him pace back and forth behind his desk. His robe shifted as if it were suddenly too big on his frame. He was not young, but not old, either. The curtains behind him draped half open, and fresh noon light filtered into the room in bright rays. They caught the edges of his receding hairline, and created deep shadows along his cheeks and mouth, making him look tired, almost pained. His blond hair took on a gray cast.

Something was wrong, and he was delaying.

"If this is about—"

"Say nothing." He held up his hand, palm out.

I had no patience anymore these last months. None. Chirl let me get away with all of my surly rancor toward my dorm-mates, and he never lectured me about avoiding parties or my old friends. He noticed everything. He said nothing. Not even about me avoiding my best friend Harly, who still did his best to be friendly to me, despite me ignoring him.

Maybe this was about my lack of social interaction? It had been months since I'd been raped. My injuries had all healed. My therapy had turned boring, though I still went to sessions which had been reduced to twice a week.

Finally, Chirl turned to face me, but he still did not meet my eyes.

What the fuck?

He took a deep breath. He put one hand on his desk, rubbing his fingers in a circle on the wood beside his prize knick-knack: a large hourglass.

His discomfort seemed to draw all the moisture from the air. My throat went dry. This drama; it was unusual.

Chirl cleared his own throat.

My muscles hardened under my skin as I sat and waited.

He cleared his throat a second time and began. "I received an email this morning."

He took a deep breath.

"About me?" I asked.

He nodded.

Of course. Orion. "I can explain--" I began.

"Hush. This is not about anything you have done."

"Oh." I waited.

"The Alpha who attacked you. If you recall, his name is Bosk."

Everything went a little blurry. The room wanted to fade, as if the whole world were a dream.

"So he emailed you? Why?" I didn't want to ask but I couldn't help myself. Someone else ruled my body and my voice sounded like it came from far away.

Chirl swallowed hard. "You know he did some time in jail for what happened. He got behavioral and medical treatment for his actions during his Burn."

"I don't really care about that." My lungs were shaking but my voice came out steady, though everything still seemed muffled, like this was all happening behind veils of layered cloth.

"He's making a claim."

"A w-what?" I prayed I did not hear that last correctly.

"A claim. On you."

"He can't do that." *Can he?* My veins went cold.

"It's legal. More, he claims he made a bond with you during the—uh--" Chirl couldn't finish.

"That's a lie!" Blood rushed in my ears. I blinked and shook my head to clear my mind.

"He's an Alpha who claims a bond and is claiming the Omega he bonded with. You. Of course you may demand a test to verify the claim, but not until after he has had a year to make sure the bond is completely and fully formed."

"A year?" I knew Alpha rules. I had learned them frontward and backward and sideways in class. Omegas had few rights, but one of them involved the Alpha claim. If the claim of bonding did not take within a year, an Omega would not be beholden to that Alpha and could go elsewhere and find a true bondmate.

But an Alpha could make a claim—a legal claim—on any unbonded Omega, even one under the guardianship of a parent or other relative, which was why they were so jealously guarded when raised in homes by families.

At the farms, we had no recourse. Any of us could be claimed. Most Alphas didn't do it unless a relationship was forming. But most Alphas weren't my attacker.

The only Omegas safe from Alpha claims were the ones who were institutionalized. They, along with Sylphs, the by-products of Omega to Omega matings, were protected under the laws.

Bosk. What a horrible name. The room grew very small. I saw myself on the floor, naked, rough hands all over me, holding me down, hitting me, bending me into impossible positions, and the body of the very large Alpha rutting into me.

The room blackened for a moment.

I felt a hand on my shoulder, gentle and heavy, and blinked upward, the blackness fading to reveal Chirl's face. He was bent a little at the waist, leaning in toward me.

"I am doing what I can to delay him. Extra paperwork. And I have contacted all my sources for advice on how to fight this and make him go away."

But I knew. Bosk wanted me. He wanted to finish what he thought he'd started. A bonding. So I would be his to abuse forever to his heart's content.

Bosk was an Alpha. The law favored him. Bosk would win.

"I have been in meetings all morning discussing this situation with Sen and others. Sen can have you committed."

"Committed?"

"Declared mentally unfit to bond. But you would be sent to an institution for the rest of your life."

My breath caught. A sudden pain rolled up through my stomach and into my chest. A voice in my head began a litany. *Your life is over. Your life is over.*

The hand on my shoulder gripped. Tight. "I will not turn you over to that man." Chirl's tone did not rise, but his every word seemed to punch the air. "I promise."

I knew he spoke his heart. He was strict but never mean.

I opened my mouth to speak but couldn't find my sound. Nothing but air came from my throat.

"There are some institutions that are very well-kept and comfortable. The more expensive ones. We don't have funds here, but I'm sure if Orion were to be informed, he'd pay. You have been a valued employee of his. He likes you."

Orion. I'd cleanly forgotten about him in these last moments.

The words *institution, Orion* and *he likes you* whirled about my brain. But more, the flashbacks nearly whited out my thoughts. That Alpha, that man who tried to tear me apart from the inside out wanted to claim me?

I would kill myself first.

Chirl's promise held no weight. He could not stand against Alpha laws. Not if the Alphas involved were rich and powerful enough. They could grab me right out of any institution if they decided Chirl lied to get me in one.

Did I even want a life inside one of those prisons? Zilly's was bad enough, but at least the Omegas I grew up with were sane.

Orion owed me nothing. I felt a fury rise up in me to think of begging any Alpha to pay for me to be safe in an institution under a pretense of any sort of altruism.

I couldn't think straight. I could barely see Chirl as he left my side and approached his desk and computer. The light all around him was white. My own hands were ice.

Chirl said, "We need to take care of this right away."

"When?" I managed to croak out.

"Today. Bosk comes at five to make his claim."

I could barely see the clock on the wall with the big black hands and the slow-moving second hand. But I knew it was around noon. Five hours. That was all the time I had. And it was nothing. Not even so much as a blink.

I don't know how long I sat in Chirl's office, my breath shallow and shaking in my chest.

"I have to go."

"Please wait." Chirl sat at his desk. I heard the wheels of his chair squeak as he moved. The tapping of a keyboard echoed about the room. Too loud. Everything was bright and confusing and loud.

"I have to—to do something. Pack, I guess." Far away, I heard my words make the reality of a sentence. But I wasn't really sure what it meant.

"Hold on," Chirl said. "I'm getting a response right now from Orion."

"What?"

"Orion says he's pulling up the claim right now and looking it over. Just wait."

"I—I have to go," I said. But my body would not move. Was I even breathing right now?

"Another message just popped in. Orion is meeting us here in one hour."

I shut my eyes. Orion was coming here. Fan-fucking-tastic. Now I had two Alphas coming to Zilly's because of me. For me.

Abruptly, I stood, opening my eyes.

"Where are you going?" Chirl asked.

Of course I didn't know. I had to stand. To move. To walk away. The world was dissolving around me. The solid floor under my feet was an illusion.

I watched Chirl pick up a house phone. He gave some orders. He hung up.

"You're staying here until this is resolved. With me. I have ordered lunch to be brought in."

"I need to go," I said.

"No." His voice came soft, but firm. He picked up a remote from his desk and flicked on the wall TV screen beneath the big round clock. "Watch TV. Don't think. Wait. You are not alone. We'll handle this. One way or another, we'll handle this."

I sat down, straight-backed, my hands in my lap. Already, I could feel the shackles. I had no control over my life. None. Decisions would be made for me. My fate rested in the hands of only those with power.

It was infuriating.

The chatter of the TV meant nothing to me. It was as if every person were speaking a foreign language. I was lost. I did not recognize my own life.

I heard Chirl tapping away at his keyboard in rapid strokes. He made phone calls and his voice hissed. I wanted to listen, to know. But my brain would not function.

Everything was over for me. I had to accept it. All around me stretched a desert with no air. My future robbed. Although I'd not had much of a future to begin with.

Chirl sat in a chair beside me and doled out lunch. I took a plate but didn't eat.

Sen came in and sat with us for a while. He spoke to me kindly but I don't know what he said. I only nodded.

But I did hear him whisper to Chirl, "He is in no shape to be claimed."

"I know," Chirl whispered back.

Wonderful, I thought. I wasn't in shape for social anything, but at least I had a job that kept me out of the way and gave me an office with a view of the pool. But not now.

I told myself I didn't care.

A knock came on the office door. I jumped at the sound. Chirl rose and went to the door.

Orion came in, followed by the older Alpha I'd seen him with months ago on his tour of Zilly's.

Orion. His presence exuded confidence and determination. He filled the room with his Alpha cologne, something expensive, no doubt, that millionaires wore.

I couldn't help but look up at him and when I did the air cleared. My mind became sharp. Every line of his face and hair, his jacket and tie, came into focus with clean edges. He wore all black, including the shirt, with a brilliant blue tie, as blue as the swimming pool my office faced.

He turned to face me and nothing else existed in the world for me but him. If I stood up and walked straight into him it would be like entering that pool I loved, immersing myself, letting the water lap up and over me to encompass me and pull me down into peace and the strength of eternity.

I blinked hard a few times, thinking I was dizzy, I was still in shock, but no. Orion's presence and his affect on me was real. It did not diminish. It grew stronger and tighter all around me.

How could I be so drawn to him in the midst of this horror show?

I hated it.

I stood and faced him. I had to look up. I was shorter but I felt all my power and rage and anger return. He grounded me enough so I had that to hold onto, as annoying as it was.

"I want you to know it wasn't me who asked you to come here today," I said.

Chirl turned to look at me with raised eyebrows.

Sen crossed his arms firmly over his chest and looked almost amused.

"No," Orion replied. "Warden Chirl asked me here. As I understand it, we have a big problem to solve."

"It's not your problem!" The words banged the air like I was an angry child.

"It is. I own Zilly's and I have made it my policy to allow no harm to come to its residents when I have the power. Today I was informed a dangerous Alpha has come to claim you. I have read that claim. He states a mate-bond was formed."

I tried not to snarl but something like a hiss escaped my lips.

"I need to hear it direct from you if you believe this is true. Do you feel a bond was formed on that day?"

I huffed. "Of course not! Never!"

"That's all I needed to hear."

"It's not enough," Chirl began.

Orion held up his hand for silence. "The law states an Alpha has one year during a legal claim to make a rightful and legal mate-bond with any Omega. I cannot get around that law, but I do have a very good lawyer."

Orion pointed to the man at his side who lifted his chin.

"This is how we handle the situation," Orion continued. "This is my attorney, Saben. He has friends in high places. He drew up a second claim for you, Holland. This claim pre-dates the claim from the Alpha Bosk. The claim is under my name, since I own Zilly's now, and feel I am responsible for everything that happens here."

I laughed. "You're making a claim on me?"

"With no strings attached, I might add." Orion looked me directly in the eye. "You have a choice. Under my protection, which starts today and will continue for one year, you can come with me and continue your work for Zilly's in an office in my home. Or you can go to an institution where you cannot be touched by another Alpha. It will be the best place money can provide, but it will still be an institution."

There was, really, no choice. "You want me to go with you?"

"If you come with me I can guarantee your safety."

He'd been making this same statement in emails over and over. But now I had no choice but to ask, "How?"

"We'll make a contract. Binding. No one touches you. Your safety from the world is my responsibility."

"But you are you claiming me, right?" This was crazy. But I could not look away from his gaze. His posture which seemed to take up a lot of room, puffed out even more. I felt like I was held down, immobile, breathing him into me until I was filled up with him and only him, my self drifting far off into the pine woods outside the farm.

"A legal claim is already drawn up, yes."

"And if you break the contract, what do I get?"

"Break the contract?"

"Well, if you can't control yourself, or if I don't like the situation, what then?" My boldness came from a place deep inside still untouched by anyone or anything. Not even Bosk had touched it. And Orion didn't have power over that flame I kept all to myself, hidden and fueled by hatred and rage.

"I will have a trust for you set aside, enough to keep you going in my home on your own for your lifespan. And I will leave. You get to live in my house—which is very lovely, by the way—forever and no one can touch you. You get whatever you want, servants, clothes, jewelry, entertainment. And no Alpha will be allowed to touch you without it being a crime. Because we have a contract. It will include a claim."

"But the claim only lasts one year."

"Yes." It was the lawyer, Saben, who spoke now. "But the mate-bond lasts forever."

I laughed again. "I won't be forming a mate-bond with any Alpha any time soon, that's for sure."

"Understood," Saben said. "But I have contacts who can arrange the proper ID cards and certifications, all legal, that will say you have. You will be protected."

"But the claim and bond will be fake?"

"It will be so no one else can ever touch you," Orion replied.

Why would he do this? For me? I couldn't find the words to ask. It was almost as if I dared not, because I wasn't ready to hear his reasons. If they were impersonal, I'd be insulted. If they were personal, I'd be disgusted.

"And you won't touch me," I said.

"No. Unless you give permission, nothing will ever happen."

"We'd have to fake it, though. The mate-bond. Everything."

"Yes."

"What's in it for you?" It was the closest I could come to asking why.

"Maybe to see you flourish again."

"No. It's more than that."

"I will get to see you. We've worked well together. You can't deny it. Maybe we can become friends."

"Is that what you want?"

"It is."

"Because you pity me?" This question was closer to the thing I dared not ask. I didn't want to know that every time he looked at me he saw a victim, like everyone else here at Zilly's.

"No. Because you test me. Challenge me. I like that. No Omega has ever done that to me."

I felt the responses of the others in the room with us, even though I didn't see them. The rustle of Chirl's robes. Sen's intake of breath. The lawyer's foot tapping once upon the polished floor.

"You'll hate being around me, I'm sure of it." I needed to deflect. I needed him to see me as something other than a ruined being. He must not see me that way, wrecked and scarred, a mere specter of my former self. I couldn't take it.

"Maybe."

"And when you get tired of me, you won't throw me back here to the farm?"

"No. I said that would be in the contract. A lifelong contract. You will always have a room at the house. It is part of the contract and part of the claim which will become binding after the mate-bond certificates are filed."

"A fake claim. A fake mate-bond."

"Yes."

"When would we do it?"

"Are you saying yes?"

I nodded, trying to stave off the eagerness to get away from Bosk and Zilly's with a slight shrug."

"My other choice is the institution, and while that holds some intrigue for me, living a life with no demands upon me, sitting in the sun with my hat over my eyes, I suppose your offer also has its benefits." I sighed as if it didn't matter. But it mattered. Too much.

Orion raised his eyebrows at my casual indifference.

"When would you like to leave, then?" His voice came clipped.

"Now." I needed to leave before Bosk arrived. I could not take seeing that Alpha again.

"This afternoon, then?"

I stuck my chin out. "That would be good for me."

Suddenly, Chirl and Sen were talking both at once.

"I'll help you get packed."

"I'll see to the paperwork."

"You will want your office computer?"

"I will contact Bosk and tell him his claim is void."

The joy with which Chirl said that last edged his tone.

"I have everything Holland will need at my home," Orion interrupted. "The computer can remain here. His uniforms will not be required attire."

Orion met my eyes.

"Whatever personal items you want to bring are fine."

I not did want to sound rushed, but now that all had been decided, I couldn't wait one more minute. "I can be ready in half an hour."

The corners of Orion's mouth flinched upward in a small, held back smile. "I will wait."

*

The container seemed small and too light to encompass a life.

It held: an old teddy bear, my tablet with pictures of my fellow Omega classmates, all the boys I'd grown up with. A few folded clothes including my new jeans, underwear and socks took up one corner. My brush and comb. My razor. My toothbrush. Some old makeup I never wore. A tiny rectangular case no bigger than my palm that played a tune when you turned the little handle. It had a jester painted on it. It had been a graduation gift from the company of Zilly's. We all got one with different pictures. A token. A knickknack that was worthless, but I'd loved it.

Harly came rushing into my room as I put the lid on my box of personal items.

"I heard you're leaving! A claim! That can't be true!"

I looked up at him, my eyes clear, and saw a happy Omega who loved the mating halls and couldn't wait to be bonded and have children. I had nothing in common with him anymore.

"It's true." I turned away to tuck the blanket tighter about my neatly made bed.

"But—"

"It's Orion and it'll be okay."

"Wow. He's so dreamy and rich. But—but you can't want this," he protested.

"It will be fine." I kept my voice level and did not look at him.

"Orion. He's a millionaire."

I swallowed hard, but nodded.

"Holland--"

"It's fine. It is what it is."

"Well, congratulations."

When I said nothing, he said, "I'll never see you again."

"I know."

"Holland, look at me."

Grudgingly, I turned and met his eyes.

"We've been friends since we could walk. I'll miss you. Won't you miss me."

I glanced away. "Sure."

"I'm so sorry about what happened to you. But this is good, right?"

"Sure." I didn't want to hear those words. It was why I avoided him. My best friend. I couldn't take pity from him, of all people.

"Holland," he said firmly. "Hey."

"What?"

"I'm going hug you. Now."

I turned back toward him. Said nothing.

"I'm going to hug you," he said again.

He came to me then, and I let him put his arms around me. It felt awful and terrible and wonderful and my throat swelled and I thought I might choke.

"You'll be okay. You promise me," he whispered in my ear. "You'll heal and be healthy and wonderful. And maybe you'll think of me now and again. Right? I love you, Holland. I love you."

Slowly, my hands raised around his waist and my palms pressed against his ribs. Harly. He'd been my brother. My confidant. My other half. Until everything got ruined.

I love you, too. I wanted to say it aloud but my throat swallowed the words.

"I know," he said softly, as I started to pull away. "I know you'll be well and have a wonderful life." He looked at me, his hands still on my waist. "I know because you're you. You're you and you always will be. Holland, the brightest, the best, the most beautiful."

I pulled away from him. My insides trembled violently. I had no structure in this moment, and I needed it.

Harly seemed to know it. And he didn't need more from me than I could give. He never had. Tears dotted his cheeks, but he smiled wide enough that his pretty, straight white teeth showed. He always had the best smiles.

"Can I carry your box out front for you?" he asked.

Biting the inside of my lower lip, I nodded. "Thank you."

Chapter Ten

Orion

The limo waiting outside the front gate, humming under the blue sky, was a giant but elegant piece of machinery that would glide us to our new arrangement.

I had wanted to drive myself in my Jeep, but I figured I needed this to look official and special. Only the best for my fake bondmate.

For an Omega who needed rescuing, Holland seemed very calm when I met him in Warden Chirl's office. But telltale signs communicated otherwise. This situation was nothing if not dire. For him to be potentially turned over to be claimed by the man who'd raped him turned my stomach. It had to be a horrific nightmare for him. It was a wonder he remained coherent.

Now as my driver loaded Holland's small box of belongings into the trunk, Holland held his head high. He walked smoothly to the open passenger door. But as I saw him touch the side of the door and lower himself to step inside, his hand trembled.

Once I entered the limo behind him and sat on the couch seat facing him, I saw the tension in the muscles around his mouth and eyes. He stared straight forward and over my left shoulder, his blue eyes bright and clear.

Many times I'd asked him in emails to meet me. For a meal. For an in-person conference. He'd always declined.

I wondered now what must be going through his mind.

He wore his white shirt buttoned all the way to his neck. His black trousers fit him loosely about the hips. He leaned back stiffly, his silken hair falling in shiny waves over one cheek, and clasped his hands in his lap.

It was just me and him in the back. Saben had driven himself to meet me at Zilly's and was long gone now to file all the paperwork.

I turned and opened the fridge. I had made sure the limo was well-stocked. I took out two beers, opened them, and handed him one.

He took it with a raised eyebrow.

"I think we both need a drink. Have you ever had a beer?"

He shook his head.

Of course not. Zilly's did not allow alcohol on the premises. I'd read that regulation several times over the past months.

I took a sip of mine.

Holland followed suit. Grimaced. Said nothing.

I smiled at his reaction. "Are you hungry?"

He lowered his lashes and his eyes actually seemed to flash. "Why?"

"Because I am."

He squinted, almost glaring. "I'm not dating you," he stated.

He was stone, but he mesmerized me.

"I understand."

Holland tilted his head. "Why did you come for me?"

"Because what happens to you matters to me."

"You rushed to the farm. Like someone was dying."

"In a sense, that's how it came across. To turn you over to that—that Alpha was a death sentence. I wouldn't allow it."

"Yet entirely legal for him to make the claim."

"Unfortunately, yes."

Holland set his beer in a cup holder by the window and rubbed at the surface of the glass bottle with one finger. "I suppose I should be all thankful and gracious."

"No. You can be however you wish. No strings. I'm used to your—uh—bluntly honest remarks. I expected nothing else."

"You mean you're used to me being rude." He continued to stare at the edge of the window.

I downed half my beer and let it sizzle through my system. I wanted him. He could sense it. He hated it. I couldn't change who I was, but I could control my behavior.

"I am used to it," I finally replied. "But the honesty is refreshing. As I've said before in countless emails, you challenge me. I'm certainly never bored when I see the light blinking a message from you."

In a soft monotone, he said, "You play the hero."

"If that's how you want to see it."

"I don't want to see it that way. You come to the rescue, and oh that's supposed to be so great. Makes you so special. But what does that make me?"

"What do you mean?" I certainly did not like where his thoughts were headed.

"It makes me nothing." He blinked, looking sideways at me. "Nothing in your eyes."

"You're not nothing. You're a human being who deserves better than what you were headed for. I saw no other recourse. I wasn't going to let that Alpha take you. Not after--"

"After what? Oh yeah. Well, my body is healed. I'm fine. You don't have to look at me like I'm some charity case."

"Never thought that." I leaned back, staring at the white leather interior of the limo's roof.

The truth had never been about charity or altruism or any nature in me to do the right thing where Holland was concerned. With all the other Omegas at Zilly's, yes, I felt those responsibilities to make life better for them. But not Holland.

The truth swelled through me, not charity, and far from innocent. But it was pure. He delighted me. I favored him. From the moment I saw him speak out on my tour of the farm, he had my attention like no one else I'd ever met, no Alpha, no Omega, no one.

Holland drew all my focus. He always had. Our eyes met over a crowded room as he demanded my identity and wanted to know why Alphas were invading his territory. He had me in that moment. He was the last thing I thought of before sleep and the first when I woke every morning.

If he knew these past months I waited poised at my computer for any messages and emails from him, he'd laugh. He'd never believe it.

As I tried to quiet the buzz of my thoughts, Holland spoke.

"How will the arrangements be? Will I have my own room?"

My heart started to beat softer. "Yes. You'll have your own room. And your own office."

"Will we take meals together?"

I couldn't help the tightening of muscles in my forehead. "I would hope."

"Hmm."

"I live alone. If you want your meals separate, fine. But it seems a waste. I'd like the company, anyway."

He stared down at his clasped hands. His beer sat fizzing softly under the window, untouched. "We aren't friends."

Harsh words, like a knife. We'd worked together for months. "I disagree."

He glanced up. Deep in the blues of his irises shone a tiny vulnerability, a paleness within the crisp light of his eyes.

"It's hard for me to be near you," he said. A finality communicated in the set of his lips.

It was hard for me to be near him as well. His scent rushed in on me, faintly salt mixed with beautifully blooming aromas of summer roses. Maybe it was a cologne he liked. But I suspected it was him because I reacted to it like an Alpha around any Omega he might fancy, my blood surging a bit faster, my skin tingling. I didn't have that response to manufactured perfumes.

But Holland's statement about being near me was for different reasons than mine. He didn't get a rush from me. He didn't even like me. Within his sweet perfume scent was a hint of bitters. He was afraid.

He showed his fear through his emotionless stance, and his rude and clipped sentences. After working with him, and our two brief encounters during the tour, I knew he would never admit to outright fear. It wasn't in his character to give in, or to show vulnerability in any way.

But everything in me responded to his situation with an urge to protect. If I admitted it, he'd hate me even more.

The limo pulled up to my favorite Italian restaurant. When the driver came around to open the door, Holland looked at me in confusion.

"I eat out a lot," I said.

"Certainly you have staff at your home. Cooks and butlers and things," he said.

"You assume a lot. But yes, I do. All inherited."

"I'd like to go there and get settled then."

"This lunch will be a stop of no more than an hour," I replied, moving out of the car and standing. A wind blew across my brow, cooling it. It was only then I realized I'd been hot.

The drive was tedious. Zilly's was an hour from my home. Holland could not complain that I wanted a break at the half-way mark.

Holland scooted forward along the leather couch and stood, glancing around the front of the restaurant and the parking lot behind us. He had an almost startled look about him, and I realized he had not been out in public a day of his life.

He took a deep breath and settled his shoulders, back stiff and chest thrust out.

"There will be all Alphas in there, right?" he asked with a toss of his head.

"Some will have their Omega mates with them. And this particular restaurant has an Omega cook that is amazing."

He nodded curtly.

It was early in the afternoon, though, so I knew the place would not be busy. Better for Holland to acclimate himself to eating out.

"And my attire?" he asked.

"You look fine."

It didn't seem to be what he wanted to hear, but he turned to face the front doors.

I led us through them. Holland stayed quite close to my side, which I tried not to enjoy too much. Truly, I didn't want him to hate me even more than he already did.

Already the aromas of lasagna, chicken parmesan and fine wines greeted us. My stomach rumbled in anticipation.

The tables all had candles flickering in orange jars. A single red rose stood in a faceted crystal vase on every red and white checkered tablecloth. Music played softly in the background.

An Alpha greeted us with a big smile, and a lot of black curls nearly obscured his vision. "Welcome! Take any seat you'd like."

Holland glanced about, then nodded toward a corner. I decided it was perfect. Privacy would be best as he learned to relax in public now that he was no longer locked away on a farm.

"That one?" I lifted my hand toward the corner as we walked toward it. "It's just fine."

An Alpha waiter brought us menus and offered us wine. Without thinking, I ordered two glasses of white.

Holland said, "Water, please." He stared at the Alpha waiter as if waiting for him to argue.

But the Alpha smiled and said, "Of course."

I had not meant to order for him. But he didn't say a word. He picked up the menu and from what I could see began at the top of the first part and read every word.

When he put the menu down, he gazed at me, his eyes tight and wary as usual. He said, "I didn't eat any of my lunch today back at the farm. So I would like to try the cheese ravioli. We have an Omega cook at Zilly's that fries it so the edges are crisp, but it's soft on the inside."

I nodded, smiling. "The ravioli here is good."

He took a breath as if about to speak, then stopped. "What?"

"If I think of the outside as just a sort of farm itself, only bigger and allowing Alphas to freely roam, I am certain I can become used to it." He glanced about the restaurant, looking at the customers at other tables. Some were Alphas, but a few Omegas sat with Alpha mates.

"They will all think we are together?" he asked.

"For all intents and purposes, I have legally claimed you. We must never speak of it as anything other than very real. You understand?"

"Yes." He swallowed. "I understand you get to play the hero once again."

Despite his cutting remark, a tiny needle-like thrill shot through my chest. The more he made an effort not to be subservient, the more he ingratiated himself to me. If he knew it was my predilection, he'd probably stop talking altogether.

"I would not have ever allowed you to be sent to Bosk," I quipped back.

He sat back, his shoulders against the chair top, his hands in his lap. The candlelight played across the angles of his face, offsetting his beauty. Shadows flitted in his eyes. His hair brushed gently against the line of his jaw.

"It's for the best. I probably would have killed him." He said the word lightly as he stared over my shoulder.

I wasn't surprised, but I could not say to him he wouldn't have survived it. He wasn't more than a hundred and thirty pounds soaking wet. I'd never met Bosk, but I'd seen the report and his photo. He was huge, larger than I. Intimidating. I couldn't imagine what Holland had been through with that Alpha.

The Alpha waiter came back to take our order then. When Holland ordered, the waiter asked him if he wanted soup or salad.

92

Holland looked taken aback, as if he'd done something wrong.

"It comes with the meal," I said by way of explanation.

"Salad," he replied, frowning upward.

"Dressing?"

"Italian."

The waiter was a small Alpha, and very friendly. He did not ogle Holland. But neither did he defer to me when asking what Holland preferred.

As far as first times out and about in the world, this was a good practice session for Holland. He could see that Alphas came in all shapes and sizes here, and that they were not all monsters wanting to rape Omegas just for breathing.

Still and unfortunately, the world had a long way to go in ensuring Omega rights. Rarely was an Omega ever seen alone in public without Alpha protection by his side. Often, it seemed to me the world of beasts was more civilized.

Despite Holland's order of water, the waiter still brought two glasses of wine.

"But you already had a beer in the limo," he said to me.

"I did."

"Do you drink a lot?" he boldly asked.

"Not really. At times I do to alleviate stress." I stared directly into his eyes.

As if in answer, Holland picked up his wine glass and took a long sip. When he set it down, he said, "Interesting. I've never had wine before, either."

"Well?"

"It tastes like a mix of things. But also dusty, almost salt-edged. I like it better than the beer."

"Better said than some wine connoisseurs I know."

I felt not a small amount of shame to again realize he'd been raised in such—well, for lack of a better word—captivity. Yet the farm was a small world to itself with gardens and a school and a gym. It was its own society where Omegas had their special activities, games, rules and social structure.

But shame suffused me. These living, breathing beings needed to live in our Alpha world, too, without confinement, fear or needing to be mate-bonded. Keeping them confined was wrong, and yet here I was, the owner of one of the most respected and high-end services for Alphas, an Omega farm.

"So," Holland said, taking another sip of wine. "How is this really going to work?"

"The claim?"

"Of course the claim. You can't just pretend forever. And then where will I be?" His eyebrows pressed so low they created shadows on the tops of his cheeks.

"I would never force a claim, you must understand that. And yes I can pretend forever. With good lawyers and enough money, the fake claim and mate-bond would never be challenged."

He gave a little huff. His face took on a no-nonsense expression. "But my position, I'm sure you can see, leaves few choices wherein I am forced to choose the least worst possible scenario. You understand that, don't you? In the end, it's still force. And I will never be free to seek a bondmate of my own. Nor will you."

"We can cross that bridge should we come to it."

The restaurant lights and candles and shadows suddenly seemed to all converge on me, rushing into my vision.

I was insulted he saw me as no better than any other Alpha who believed Omegas were useful only as mates. I could not exclude the fact that he was attractive, or that I responded to him deep inside in not so altruistic ways, but I could control that. I thought I'd done a pretty good job of concealing said attraction, and keeping true to my own deep-secret pact of never showing him anything but pure motives.

I'd sworn my whole life never to take advantage of any Omega the way some Alphas seemed to. The way they talked and swaggered, all cock and no brain.

Despite my dad's ethically questionable business practices of owning an Omega farm, I had been raised with standards, morals and manners. Perhaps everything we did in our society was about identity, or lack thereof, and wearing masks to fit in, to protect ourselves, or to feel good about ourselves was learned. But it wasn't all pretend. I was a good person. And in all my thoughts of a future that might include a family and love, I never dreamed of wanting a mate who didn't love me in return.

"First and foremost, I need to say this. If you don't already know it. I will never disrespect you. I will never *force* you into anything."

"Hmm." Holland again glanced about the room. "It's simple. I have a year's reprieve, then, until Bosk comes to challenge your claim, demand a blood test I will not pass, and collect me."

I had already thought about all the angles. Did he think I hadn't? But I knew him from his emails. Holland liked lists. He liked organization. Right now, he was adrift.

"As I said, the blood tests can be faked. We have time. Right now, try to relax."

"Ah, relax. A simple solution not quite so easily achieved. Fake claims and blood-tests can be discovered. How can I not think about what might be coming for me? Even now?"

He was right.

"If it comes right down to it, I can hide you forever," I said. "I have ample funds. Bosk would never find you."

"And I'd continue to be a prisoner." He nodded.

"Not my first choice. But I'll do whatever it takes. I will not turn you over to him."

"It's exotic to think of being a criminal for the rest of my life."

What could I say? Was that sarcasm? With Holland, who could tell? And how could I tell him without looking like a besotted fool that I would do anything for him? Even something criminal.

Where that had come from, I didn't know. But it was the truth.

Our food came soon after his glib statement, and gave me an excuse not to reply.

Holland ate about half his meal. As preoccupied as I was with having Holland come to live with me, I still managed to eat most of mine. And indulge in a second glass of wine.

Back in the limo, with a sack between us of Holland's leftover food which he'd insisted he wanted wrapped up to go and not wasted, the air felt humid and cloying despite the air conditioner.

We glided down the road facing another half hour of sitting in silence before we reached my driveway.

I could have Bosk killed.

The thought came on fast. It was not out of nowhere. Who could help but think the world would be better without those like Bosk in it?

My discomfort traveled to my extremities, forcing me to resettle my weight in my seat.

Holland glanced at me, eyes heavy, as if he'd read my thoughts.

He hated me, no question, and there was nothing I could do about it.

Chapter Eleven

Holland

The knot of coldness in me would not retreat.

It had been almost seven months since I'd been attacked. It was April, still spring, but the jeweled eye of summer was approaching and I saw it clearly in the foliage that surrounded Orion's long drive that led to his massive house. It was his father's house, I knew, but his now, not really his choice. He'd told me as much in the things he'd revealed to me as we shot emails and messages back and forth to each other online for months.

Seeing the blooming bougainvilleas in their ecstatic pinks, and the oleanders with their soft white and rosy-pale flowers did nothing to warm me. The jacarandas dripped idle purple nearer to the front of the house. They couldn't penetrate me.

The brat I felt unfolding within me looked for a pool.

I said it again, through gritted teeth this time. "It's so big. Which wing is mine?"

Looking unperturbed, Orion leaned forward. "The house is huge. You will have your own room." He chuckled. "Yes, your own wing, if you want it."

I felt my eyebrows rise. I cocked the left one higher in a casual indifference I did not feel but needed to project to keep my sanity. I liked the idea of my own room, of course, but not my own wing. Alone in many halls gave me the creeps. I'd always been surrounded by others wherever I went on the farm, often searching for non-occupied corners in which to sit alone, but still not really alone.

I rolled my eyes to show I didn't care. But I spoke roughly to communicate my will. "Never mind my own wing. We'll have to interact. We'll have to show your servants a unified pairing. Surely you do not trust them all not to gossip."

He sat silent, gazing at me.

"So, if there's a room next to yours that is empty?" I let my last word trail off as a not-quite question. But it was a question.

"There is," he replied. "And I can have an office set up on the first floor for you within a day."

It was too much. He was giving me everything. But I wasn't about to turn any of it down. If I showed ingratitude, it was only because I didn't want to completely freak out.

So what if he gave me rooms and stuff to put in them. It was nothing to him. He was filthy rich. He could afford it and never miss the money. It wouldn't take away from his time because he'd hire people to bring furniture in, paint and tile, or whatever.

I knew he cared about what happened to me, but I kept having to tell myself none of this really mattered to him. It was an easy fix, a way for him to help a less fortunate Omega and look good doing it.

But he did care. And I couldn't take that. So for me it was best to operate as if I myself didn't.

But the errant thought kept coming back, one I wanted to wipe away. If things had been different, he might have been someone I could feel something with. He was my type, certainly, and played into all the fantasy stereotypes I had as a youth for mating and family.

I blinked hard. I wouldn't think it. I couldn't. The wreck of me that remained after the attack still lay about me in bloody pieces. It was my right now to hate all Alphas. I'd earned it.

"You have it figured out, then, that we must show unity," he said softly. "And will you be able to hold hands with me in public?"

My face heated. "Of course."

I wanted to prove to myself that I could. That it would feel like nothing. So I reached out just as the limo stopped by the front door and grabbed his hand.

The driver got out and walked to the passenger door.

I pressed my thumb and fingers against the outside of his palm, like a pinch.

He moved his hand a little until he could grip mine in a more comfortable clasp.

He was the first to leave the car. He did not let go, but pulled me out and alongside him.

Together, hand in hand, we faced the giant, three-story abode.

His palm felt hot against my skin. But it was all right, not awkward or strange. Just a hand. A tiny part of me deep inside warmed to feel it, as if I were suddenly safe and nothing could touch me in that moment.

I looked up, breathing it in, the huge structure, the columns of the porch, the way the roof peaked into an A shape and sported a curlicue trim.

On the front side of the house, above the porch, two balconies jutted out, one on the third floor, and one on the second just above the porch roof. They were adorned with potted plants of all sizes.

I heard something rustle in the grass beyond the pathway and turned to see a black cat slink around the corner of the steps. I'd never seen a cat face to face before.

"Snowball," said Orion softly.

The cat looked up at him with big gold eyes, then flicked its gaze to me.

"You inherited him, too?" I asked.

"No. He's mine."

"I should have figured. Naming a black cat Snowball."

He shrugged. "Every name I thought up for him sounded like every other cat I'd ever met or read about. Midnight. Nightmare. Shadow. Night. I was a teenager when he came to us as a stray kitten."

Another stray. Like me. Of course it was Orion's cat. His dad would have let him keep it, and when Orion moved away the cat simply stayed. "He's old, then."

"Ah, he's got a few more years left in him."

A pang of sadness wavered in my chest. I wanted to go to the cat and pick him up, hold him until the pain inside me vanished.

Orion squeezed my hand.

I looked up at him. "What?"

"Nothing. You can pet him. He's friendly."

I glanced down. Not yet. Not so fucking much yet.

"I want to see where I'll be sleeping."

"All right."

Orion led me into the house, still holding my hand. Two servants, both smaller Alphas, rushed up and offered to take his jacket. Behind us, the driver entered with my box of personal items. One of the servants took it from him.

Orion said, "You can bring that up to the guest room next to mine. We're headed there."

"Yes, sir."

The inside of the house glistened and gleamed with marble tile and columns and gilt frames with abstract artwork inside. Two big crystal chandeliers cast brilliant light in the foyer and the large front room. A huge staircase with polished wood steps faced us. A rectangular, wooden table stretched along the entry wall. More beautiful furniture spilled across the big room before us: plush green and blue chairs, a long white couch, high tables with ornate lamps.

The air smelled of wood polish and faintly of lemons.

I pulled my hand from Orion's grip and turned to face him.

"You live here alone?"

"Not alone." He shrugged. "There's a staff."

"I know you said your dad is dead, but what about your Omega-dad?"

"An accident. He died in a fall when I was two."

"Sorry, I didn't know."

100

"Now you do."

Frowning, I tried to take it all in. Orion headed for the stairs, pulling me along. He was going too fast. I needed to wrap my mind around this.

I could see beyond the staircase a hallway that seemed to go on forever. I was used to big complexes. The farm was pretty huge, but the hundreds who lived there filled up all the space. I had my own room, but it was eight by ten feet and nothing special. But this—

"You inherited all this?"

Orion turned on the bottom step. "Yes. You know I did six months ago. You coming?"

"But it's so big--"

"Yeah, it's kind of huge. I thought about selling the place, but I grew up here. I got used to it."

"It echoes," I said.

"I know. Come on."

The Alpha servant holding my box had also paused. He said nothing and kept his gaze averted from us.

I had never been around Alphas. Now I had Alpha servants? I wondered what made me safe from them? But I wasn't going to ask in front of them.

I quickly followed Orion up the wide, long steps to the second floor. Down a wide hall, I saw at least six doors. He opened the first.

"This is my room," he said, leaving the door open and going to the next.

When he opened the second door, he said, "This is your room."

I glanced at the servant, realizing we weren't playing our claim game too well. Orion saw my nervous glance.

"It is yours to decorate and do with as you please. Your personal space. But of course you will be sleeping in my room."

It sounded all wrong but a tingle ran up my spine at the statement.

"Sir, where would you like your personal items?" the servant asked me.

Orion replied before I could answer. "For now, put them in Holland's room, please."

The servant entered and put the box on a table by a huge window leading to a balcony. "May I help you unpack?" he asked, again looking down, never at my face.

"No."

"Thank you, Alston," Orion said to him. "You can go."

I stood in the center of the room looking at the bed. It had a dark blue canopy. The walls and curtains were a paler blue, and the plush rug at my feet was black. As I looked about, I saw a door leading to a bathroom. I could see the dark marble counter and gold faucet at the sink with big mirrors along the wall. Another door, still closed, I assumed led to a closet.

Orion approached the window and slid it back a bit, letting in fresh air.

I could see the balcony beyond it. It was one of the two twin balconies that jutted from the front of the house. He turned to me.

"You may do as you please here. If you want to decorate, you may. You'll have, of course, an unlimited budget. And it's not because I'm trying to buy you. It's simply that if you decide to re-do the room, I would like it done right, with the best of materials."

"I don't know anything about decorating," I said.

"Hire help."

"Alpha help," I said.

"Not everything on the outside is Alpha run. Well, most everything is. But some Alphas run businesses with their Omega mates. It's done. Hire a couple to come in. A mated couple would never be a danger to you."

Danger. That was always on my mind. "That reminds me, I meant to ask you about your servants. You said you would guarantee my safety. But they are all Alphas."

"Yes, and they are all mated. Happily. I assure you."

I hadn't thought of that. No single Alphas worked here, then. I would be safe. The only unmated Alpha was Orion himself.

"My servants are instructed to treat you as they would me. With utmost respect."

"Already? I've only just arrived and you already instructed them?"

"I had a lot of time on the drive to Zilly's to message them all as to the new addition to my household."

"Before you even knew I'd say yes?" I quipped. "Thorough."

"Always," he answered almost curtly. "They understand I have made a claim."

"A fake claim," I muttered.

"No one will ever have to know that part of it."

He lowered his eyelids and gazed out the window. The view was spectacular: rolling lawns and big trees, a gazebo, and yes there was a pool off to the side. My pool now, for this was to be my home.

Orion said, "Yes, no one will ever have to know."

All this still meant I stood in the way of him dating, or finding a real mate. Forever, if it turned out that way. We needed to talk about this more.

Guilt clawed through me. I hated feeling that when I was the one who still had no rights. "I didn't ask you to claim me."

He swung his hands behind his back. "I am well aware of that."

He moved closer to me. I almost backed up but Orion looked down at me with a gaze gone soft in the late afternoon light. His hand came up as if to touch me, but stopped within inches of my arm.

"I want you to hear me," he said firmly. "I will never hurt you."

I turned my head away.

"Holland."

He said my name calling my attention back to him. When I flicked my gaze back up to his dark eyes, he said it again. "I will never hurt you."

I stood dumbly in the center of the room. I could think of no reply.

It seemed he waited for a good ten seconds. When I remained frozen, voiceless, his words echoing like already broken promises in my head, he turned abruptly and strode from the room.

Over his shoulder, he called, "My cook likes to serve dinner at seven."

I had wanted to discuss this more, but obviously he didn't.

With his presence gone, the air immediately cooled around me. The walls seemed to undulate. Dizzy, still in shock at my new surroundings, I sat hard on the edge of the foot of the bed. The softness of the covers bunched up around my thighs.

He'd given me too much. He was everything I ever could have wanted six months ago. Before Bosk. He would have been my fantasy come true. But now all I could think of was keeping him at bay. Remaining cold and aloof and unlikable.

So why was he compelled to keep me safe?

*

I couldn't find the dining room.

When I came downstairs, I blinked at all the brightness. I saw again the huge front room, and the long shining hall that seemed endless.

I smelled food from the kitchen, but where was it? Where was the dining room?

Starting down the hall, I saw no one about, which was a relief because I did not want to see any Alpha walking toward me, even a servant.

Hearing footfalls behind me, I turned to see Orion and a bit of my heaviness lifted. He wore a blue dinner jacket and black slacks. His unruly brown hair was slicked back and he looked—well—stunning.

"The dining room is this way," he said calmly.

We continued to walk down the hall and as it curved it opened to an area with windows all along one side and buffet tables lining the long back wall where it curved into a large hearth. Before the hearth was a couch.

A huge table that could have easily sat eighteen people took up the center dining space.

The table was already set, tall candles flickering in the shine of the plates. At one end sat a large basket of bread and rolls, butter and cream at each plate, and wine glasses with the wine already poured.

I'd had wine at lunch and it had done nothing for me except maybe make me a little more unfiltered in my speech. I didn't need that. But I eyed it with longing. The wine at lunch had been pretty good, a luxury I'd never had before.

Orion pulled out a chair at the end of the table and motioned me to sit.

I hesitated. At the farm, no one sat at the heads of the boys' tables. At the tables of the Omega workers, the head of their table was always reserved for Warden Chirl.

"Go ahead, sit," Orion said. "I'll sit here."

He pulled out the first chair on my right, close by, and sat.

Immediately, two Alphas wearing tuxedos came out from a door I had not previously seen, carrying trays.

It was more formal than anything I was used to.

I wanted to laugh. I wanted to get up and go back to my room with a sandwich or maybe just a piece of fruit. I was used to communicating with Orion through typed words. Not face to face. Lunch had been hard enough.

An Alpha servant leaned over me and I stiffened. But all he did was place a bowl of creamy soup in front of me.

I saw Orion pick up a pepper grinder and season his. When he was done, he offered it to me.

"Pepper?"

"Do you always eat this formally?" I did not take the pepper.

"My dad's servants are used to serving dinners this way. And I was brought up here. But breakfast and lunch are more like buffets. I often eat out so I don't have to endure the pomp and circumstance." He gave me a long-suffering smile. "When I was a kid I didn't know any different. But as I got older, it was boring, and now, well, I've been eating alone most of the time and it's tedious. So I go out."

"Don't you have friends?"

He looked down at his soup, taking in another spoonful. "Yes. I do. I eat with them several times a week. And you? Will you miss them?"

I picked up my spoon and stirred my soup. "No."

It was untrue. Harly had been my friend as far back as I could remember. I had been cruel to him since the attack. But I did miss him.

The steam from the soup rose up into my face, warming my eyes.

Orion picked up the basket of rolls. "Would you like one?"

I picked up a roll and put it on the smaller plate next to my wine glass.

"You're very polite. Why?"

"You're my guest. I want you to feel at home here."

"I'm your claim. More than a guest."

"Yes, but fake claimed."

Why did that make me bristle? It was not like I wanted it to be real.

"And this will be your home," Orion continued. "But as for me being polite, it was ingrained in me from an early age."

"I'll bet you don't even use the word *fuck* for the actual act, let alone slang."

"I—I don't usually use that word."

106

"That's what happens, I guess, when you're uber-rich and home-schooled."

He raised his eyebrows. "You're saying I am un-cool?"

"No. You're an Alpha. You're the cool half of the world's population by virtue of being born without internal egg sacks and a baby pouch. It's automatic. Plus, you're wealthy. It's impossible for you to be seen in any way that is not cool. You rule." I couldn't keep the sarcasm from threading through those last words.

He sighed.

I finally scooped some soup on my spoon and shoved it into my mouth.

It was heaven. I'd never tasted anything so decadent and good. Cheesy with a hint of bacon and a bit of parsley sprinkled on top.

When I swallowed, my eyes automatically closed in pleasure.

His voice intruded. "Good?"

Better than good. But aloud, I said, "It's fine."

I had not intended to be a glutton, but I saw the bottom of the soup bowl in a very short time.

Soon, the salad course was delivered.

I was already full by the time we got to our steaks, which melted in the mouth; I could only eat half.

Dessert came after, orange and lime sherbet served in cold, polished silver cups.

Both my hands went to my stomach when we were done, pressing down on the fullness there.

Orion smiled.

It wasn't that I went hungry at the farm. Far from it. We were fed three squares every day, and put on exercise schedules to remain fit. But the food there was simpler. And though Omegas cooked for us and served it, it wasn't formal but more cafeteria style. It was plain and simple food, and shared with a bunch of other squirming, hungry Omegas who could often be loud and obnoxious even though we were taught otherwise.

This was—well—snobbier. And my dinner partner was definitely a snob, rich and highly educated, as privileged as they came. Orion. Who kept smiling at me. Who kept being too infernally polite.

A voice in my head stated firmly, *If not for him you'd be with Bosk now. Only two hours ago, at five pm, he would have come for you and dragged you away forever.*

I hated that inner whisper. Any attraction I felt for Orion, or any affection—that was a no. A big no. I was glad to be away from Bosk, but any more pity from Orion-the-hero and I'd explode. If I didn't seem thankful enough, it was because it wasn't enough. Nothing was enough for an Omega in this world until we gained rights. Until we were truly free and lived without fear.

Hell would freeze over before that happened.

Call me an ingrate. But tell me I'm not wrong.

That's what I kept saying to the mumbles inside my head.

Chapter Twelve

Orion

I knew it from the moment I first saw him at Zilly's. There was a lot of armor on that one. I very well understood what I was getting into when I made my offer to fake-claim Holland. His spitefulness, his curt disrespect, his insolent hatred of Alphas—why did that intrigue me so? And his startling beauty—it burned straight through my mind.

Was I that bored? So privileged that anything outside my scope of "normal" was exotic?

I could be that shallow, I decided. But I didn't want to be. No matter what, something about Holland made me want to protect him. That was first and foremost in my thoughts. He could hate me forever, and I'd still feel that urge. If it never turned into more for him, and probably it wouldn't, I would live knowing he was okay, for I had protected him.

I thought about going back to my office after dinner. There was always work; it was never done. But when I noticed Holland following me—not too close but still there—I turned toward my game room where I had a huge flat screen TV, half a dozen antique pinball machines, air hockey, a pool table, and a sleek, fully stocked bar.

It wasn't that I wanted to take up drinking. But alcohol was one of those things that relaxed me in college. I'd never been into weed or hard drugs, so that was what I thought of when I needed to calm myself down.

Holland continued to follow me. "Do I get a tour of the place?" he called out just as I opened the door.

"Tomorrow," I answered. Then I stood in the doorway, and let him enter first.

His eyes widened. His smooth cheeks glimmered in the flickering lights. He'd shaved before dinner. He looked sharp-edged and perfect.

"We have a pool table at Zilly's," he commented, glancing at my table in the center of the room.

"Let's play."

I hadn't played in years. In college, we did more outdoor sports to cool off our youthful energy.

To my surprise, Holland, with his cool and precise control, wiped the mat with me on every game.

He made me laugh, just because he was so good, though I barely saw him crack a smile. That presence he had, so raging, so full of what he wanted but thought he could never have, took up the entire room. He was maybe five six. Maybe a hundred and thirty pounds. I was six-three and two hundred pounds. But sometimes he made me feel small, and to catch up with him I wanted to give him stuff. Give him everything.

In almost every sense, I had. He would never go hungry. He would live here always, or wherever the money I gave him access to took him.

When he wasn't aware, my eyes would draw down his body and imagine the scars he might have. I had read the reports. The broken bones, the sprains, the bruises, the abrasions. What about scars unseen but still there? It made me crazy to think about it as I watched him bend to finish yet another game as he sacked the eight-ball.

"That's it!" I clapped him on the back.

He jumped, but took it without comment, his small body barely giving way. I had been gentle but thoughtless, forgetting he might hate any touch.

I had never been anything but a gentleman with any Omega.

But his chin came up and he acted as if my little smack had never happened at all.

We moved on to air hockey. Then ping pong.

We finished the night with beers, some pinball, and a fast action movie.

We didn't really talk much but it was nice to have company. His company. Hell, I'd lived for his emails and messages.

"So," he said. The hour was late. "When am I getting my office?"

"You will. Everything has been ordered to be delivered tomorrow. It will be set up by noon."

"We work. We play. It's a life." His tone came out low, almost clipped.

"It's good to have someone else living here." He had to know I liked him.

He turned toward me. His perfect stance, hair, clean unwrinkled clothes, demeanor all unruffled. But inside, what must he be thinking, feeling?

He was displaced. Surrounded by Alphas now, the enemy. All strangers.

"You do know you are allowed to have friends visit. From Zilly's. Plan ahead and we'll send a car."

He shrugged as if to brush off my offer.

"I want to know," he began. Stopped. Started again. "I want to know if others can detect it. The claim. If they can tell it's fake."

"The scent changes with a bond but mainly for the couple alone. Certainly you know that. But a claim is paperwork only."

"Oh." He took a deep breath until his chest puffed up.

"What? Ask me anything."

"Bosk said he'd made a bond with me. Doesn't that supersede a claim? Any claim? Even one with fake blood tests showing a mate-bond?"

"I will be honest. If his bond is true, it would. But you have no feeling of it. So it must be a lie."

He bowed his head.

It was a legitimate worry. It was no surprise these questions were on his mind.

"Tell me," I said. "Do you feel anything?"

"There was no bond. How could there be? All I ever knew was fear and pain. It couldn't happen. It takes two, doesn't it?" He glanced up, then down again. He turned and picked up his beer, shaking the bottle and finding it empty.

"Yes. Your scent would change. And the blood samples taken to prove a mate-bond show in the testing."

"How?"

"You sound unsure about Bosk's claim. Is that why you are asking?"

"No. But I need to be sure there isn't some trick up his sleeve. I need to know."

"I've never had a mate-bond. What I've read you've probably read, too. You experience feelings of love, propriety, unusual rapport. You've seen the movies just like I have. The mated pair feel it when the other dies. My dad felt it. He knew my Omega-dad died before he was informed."

"That's very sad."

I nodded. "It was a bad time, though I barely remember it."

We were going to have to talk about this subject a lot if we were to show the world our united pairing. But right now my tiredness was getting to me. It'd been a long day.

"I don't feel Bosk, except blind rage. Hatred. I try not to think about him at all."

"I've never heard of a—well—a hate-bond forming."

He tilted his head. "That's good. Real good. One way of putting it. But what if—I keep thinking—"

I shook my head to reassure him. "It can't be possible, I would think. A bond forming through violence, just—no. And you said you don't feel anything."

"I feel hate. I wouldn't care if he died. And my scent is the same as far as I know. But what if the doctors didn't know, or Chirl knows but never said anything? Where would that leave me?"

"It's not a concern because it didn't happen."

Bosk. He was going to be the star of our nightmares tonight.

"I think I should get a private blood test. Very private. I want to be sure."

It was a bad idea. I could feel it. That what-if horror that it might be true, and that Holland couldn't feel it because his rage blocked it.

He had to be terrified to be thinking this now. Bosk had claimed him only hours ago. What a jolt. And now, this unsecured feeling that just maybe the monster had a legitimate claim that would supersede mine—my fake claim. Our fake mate-bond papers which were still being created.

"We can get you tested tomorrow. I'll hire a private facility. For our eyes only."

He nodded. A shine came over his eyes. And I knew. He was scared. He would never show it, though.

"If you need anything. You cannot be afraid to come to me. Any time, day or night."

"A good night's sleep. That's what I need," he replied, and he tossed his hair to one side so its gleaming ends trailed along his neck and shoulder. His dark hair wasn't long, but it was past his ears, and it moved when he moved his head, sliding in silken strands against his ears, his jaw, and sometimes over his eyes.

I took a step toward him and his head came up fast.

"You may not believe it," I said. "But I do want to be your friend. I know me being an Alpha makes that nearly impossible, but I'm not Bosk. I know what friendship means. I know what loyalty means. I know how not to break a promise. And how to take care of my own. You are an Omega from Zilly's. I own Zilly's. That makes you part of my family."

"No. I'm part of your business." Those dark blue eyes shone with a sudden flame and deeper beyond that heat, shadows upon shadows.

"That's not how I think of you."

"Then how do you think of me? As some unfortunate who got ruined by a crazy Alpha? Yeah, that's what you will always see when you look at me!"

"No. Family." I spoke that last word with conviction, my throat pushing it out with a hard breath.

"What?" He laughed with no mirth. "Like a brother? A cousin?"

More, I wanted say. *Much more.* "Whatever you like. But more, after these months of working together, a friend. I don't expect you to want to feel friendship for me. I'm an Alpha and you hate us. I understand. But I truly feel that toward you. So you are part of my family whether you like it or not since you can't control my feelings."

He looked like he was about to stomp his foot. He controlled himself better than that, though. "And now you probably want me to thank you."

"No. I said no strings. No thanks are necessary. But Holland, understand this. I won't let that man near you. Ever."

His chin went down. We were both so tired. The day had started wrong and now we were here with Holland displaced and me trying to play the hero without acting like a hero.

"We both need sleep. We have time to figure out all of this."

"Not if he really produced a mate-bond."

"We have a year at worst. No one knows. He's a big mouth. He brags. He is mentally ill. And an ex-con. No one will believe him. We have time."

He puffed air from his nose and turned away.

"Believe it, Holland. We have time!"

"Whatever."

That night, we climbed the stairs to our rooms in silence.

It wasn't a good start to our cohabitation, but it was a start.

Chapter Thirteen

Holland

My first night at Orion's ostentatious house was both good and bad.

Orion sucked at pool and ping pong, and it felt good to beat him.

I luxuriated in my new bed. And there was a swimming pool I looked forward to visiting.

But the bad parts were bad. First, I was surrounded by unknown Alphas. He promised his servants were mate-bonded Alphas, but how could I be sure?

As the evening wore on, I kept thinking about Bosk's claim of a bond. What if all of Orion's money and lawyers and our fake claim couldn't stand up to it? What if it was real and I had blocked it out?

I tossed and turned that night, the sheets soft and warm, my beautiful room in Orion's estate a great gift I could not deny. But I kept thinking about taking the blood test. If Bosk was bonded to me, we could never fake a mate-bond even with all the proper paperwork in place because he would have his own blood test to refute my fake bond with Orion. To be sure, I needed and wanted the test. But I was so scared of the outcome I kept having to remind myself to breathe. No luxury could help me. No powerful and wealthy Alpha could stand against their own laws.

It was as if Bosk were attacking me all over again. I was afraid to search my thoughts in case I found some feeling there, some residual sense of him that had infected my flesh and blood to form an invader in my mind.

What did nature and the law do for unwanted mate-bonds?

I was jumping ahead of myself, as I often did when worrying details. Even as a kid, I had trouble sleeping the night before school exams.

I thought about getting up and searching the subject online, but my working computer was back at my office at Zilly's, and my tablet with my personal belongings had been off all day. I hadn't synched it to Orion's Wifi yet, and I certainly wasn't going to wake him for the code.

Feeling helpless, I tossed and turned. It wasn't until the faintest early light shone through the curtains that I finally dropped off to a dreamless sleep.

*

I found the dining room by myself in the morning.

Orion, hair hastily tamed, clothed in his usual black suit, was already sitting at the table flicking through something on a tablet as he drank a steaming cup of coffee. He looked too damn perfect.

The cat I'd seen on my arrival yesterday sat in one of the dining room chairs licking its paw and ignoring everything else in the room.

Snowball. The black cat.

I saw food on the sideboards set out buffet style and began helping myself to scrambled eggs and bacon.

Orion glanced up when he heard me rattle a dish.

"Good morning."

There was nothing good about it. I'd had maybe three hours of sleep.

I poured myself some coffee and took my plate to the head of the table where I'd sat at dinner. I was grateful to see no sign yet of the Alpha servants.

"Did you sleep well?" Orion asked.

"Not really, no."

He leaned forward. "I'm sorry. Is there anything I can do?"

"This fake claim. I don't trust it."

116

"I have the best resources money can buy. It's back-dated and no one will ever question it. I know you're worried about his claim to the mate-bond, but ours will hold up."

"I am damn well worried! I want that fucking blood test!"

He sat back, staring at me. "Yes, I know. I just now made an appointment."

He turned his tablet to face me. I saw the name of a doctor at the top of the screen and a note that said: *4 pm.*

Orion leaned forward, his dark eyes flickering with warm brown highlights. "You're safe with me. Whatever I have to do I will do to keep you safe. Would you like it in writing?"

Whatever he had to do? Did that include marking me with his own scent?

But of course not. Orion was a gentleman Alpha. He'd never do such a thing, especially to someone like me who was already ruined. Broken. I knew he liked me, but anything beyond that could never happen. I wouldn't allow it. And despite him saying he wanted to be my friend, we didn't really know each other.

"I haven't even seen the claim."

"I emailed it to you but your new computer isn't set up yet. You'll have it this afternoon."

He thought of everything. To keep from looking more like a fool, I dived into my food, which was wonderful and fresh, but still crumbled like dust in my mouth.

"This afternoon, we'll drive out to see the doctor and have him run the test, then we'll have dinner out somewhere. We won't know the results for a day." His voice, as always, remained calm.

I grunted as I methodically cleaned my plate.

Alphas out of control. Lack of Omega rights. Omegas being hurt, even killed. Omegas kept as chattel. The problems of the world were huge, making my own seem so petty. I felt no mate-bond. Besides, if I ever saw Bosk again, somehow I'd find a way to kill him.

The rest of the morning was far from boring and for a while I forgot about my exhaustion and the doctor's appointment.

I supervised while furniture including a new desk, chair and couch were brought into a bare downstairs room Orion had appointed as my office. A big set of boxes arrived which I saw to be a new computer with a huge flat screen. I would have settled for a laptop, but Orion had ordered a top of the line desktop with, I soon discovered, internal and external hard drives. When I opened another box I saw he'd ordered me a new laptop as well.

I quenched my guilt, knowing it was nothing to him to pay for this stuff, and set about getting everything in order. It took hours, for which I was grateful, in that it distracted me from my immediate problems.

Orion came by occasionally to check on the progress. He gave me permission to order any decorations I wanted online, then handed me a phone and a platinum Visa.

"These are yours. The Visa's unlimited. Just don't go buying exotic pets with it or something, at least unless you check with me first. But anything else is fine."

"Even a Porsche?"

"Even a Porsche."

"I don't have a driver's license."

He waved his hand as if it didn't matter. "Hire a driver."

Anything could be mine simply by using the Visa. I stared at the card in my hand, and the phone. Things. He was giving me too many things. But I was in the outside world now. I needed them.

There was way more to this than met the eye. I wasn't just a valued employee. Orion wanted to be *friends*.

I kept running it over and over in my mind. How rude I was and continued to be. He could only be feeling sorry for me, because what was left of me to like? It made my chest burn in pain to think it.

"Do you have a gym?" I asked.

"Of course. Fully furnished. Third floor. It has a glass ceiling."

I needed to punch a bag. Or run. Or something. I didn't have time today, but it was good to know the gym was there for my use at any time.

The rest of the hours before we were to leave for the blood draw I spent setting up the rest of my office, with a short break for lunch where I made a sandwich at the buffet of offerings and ate it at my new desk.

By three o'clock, Orion came by to say we should think about leaving.

The day was clear, mid-spring, and a depthless blue sky stretched over the estate. Birds flew in dark arcs toward the horizon. Everything was bright and alive and singing with life.

My stomach rumbled but not from hunger. Nerves threatened to deplete all my energy. All the what-ifs. I couldn't fathom them.

The limo rumbled softly. We sat in leather luxury.

The drive took us on winding, pretty roads but before long we entered a freeway. I'd never been driven anywhere except the hospital when I was hurt—and I'd been unconscious then—until yesterday, and the freeway seemed fast and unsafe. Too many cars.

I gripped the edges of my trousers until my knuckles were white and kept my gaze turned toward the window, my heart trembling.

Orion might have offered me another beer but the stipulations were I could have food but no alcohol before the test.

"Would you like some water?" he asked.

Orion really was too sweet for an Alpha, let alone an Alpha who owned an Omega farm. And oh, how polite he was.

I shook my head.

"We won't know the results until tomorrow," he said. "So you can relax."

"It only makes things worse," I muttered. "This waiting."

Though the limo windows were dimmed, the light still hurt my eyes.

"We'll go back tomorrow for the results."

"In person?"

"They won't give them over the phone. I don't know, policy or something," he replied.

The city stretched before us, a gray silhouette of towers that seemed unreal. Sure, I'd seen photos of cities, but the real thing was almost alien and obtrusive. The limo took us through a tunnel and straight into the city until I lost perspective and all I could see were busy streets and buildings on either side of me.

We stopped in a parking garage. Orion and I got out into an atmosphere of gas fumes and burnt oil and went to an elevator—another new contraption for me—and took it to the seventeenth floor.

I did not know how high that was in measurements, but too high for me. Way too high. I wanted to throw up.

Once we stepped out of the elevator, however, the carpeted floors and bright lights encased us. There was no sensation of being high up any longer. A reception desk stood at the end of a small room and Orion walked up to it without hesitation.

I could not believe the person who sat behind that desk. An Omega! I could smell his lavender and silk scent.

He said, "Mister Callahan?"

"Yes."

"You have an appointment for your Omega, Holland, is that correct?"

"Yes."

I watched the small conversation unfold with ease. The Omega did not seem nervous at all to be talking to an Alpha. In fact, in his job, he seemed perfectly well-trained and at ease. And safe.

The Omega stood and led us to a door that opened onto another hall.

"You may go on in. First room on the left, please."

I looked up at Orion. "You're going with me?"

"It's our policy that Omega patients are accompanied to the exam rooms," the Omega receptionist replied before Orion could speak. "If you would like privacy, you may ask him to wait outside."

"Not necessary," I grumbled.

The Omega continued to give us his pretty smile. He was all done up, every hair in place, his suit perfectly fitted and a dash of makeup in all the right places. Beside him, I felt like a slob.

"You will be treated with the utmost respect, privacy and dignity," the Omega assured me. "The doctor is my husband and I can assure you he is the best at what he does."

Nothing but the best for Orion. He would not have hired anyone less talented or educated.

Orion and I entered the room, which was a typical doctor's office exam room with a couple of chairs, a counter with a sink, and an exam table with sterile paper covering it. I had been in enough of these types of rooms in the past months to be utterly sick of them.

"This doctor doesn't just do blood tests," I observed aloud.

"No. He is my doctor and the very best. He will take the blood and do the test himself."

"Oh."

Orion took a chair. I sat on the table with my feet hanging off. In a very short time, an Alpha male entered. He looked young but his hair was gray at the sides and pulled back in a tail. He wore a white lab coat.

"Orion! Good to see you!" He held out his hand and the two Alphas shook as if they were old friends.

"What is going on? You have an Omega you want tested for a mate-bond?"

"Yes?"

"And he's not bonded to you."

"No." Orion caught my eye. "He's from Zilly's."

"Ah yes, you are the owner now. I heard about your father and I'm so sorry."

"Thank you."

"So you inherited the farm and this Omega is from there?" The doctor turned his head, addressing me now.

"Yes," I swallowed.

"I'm Doctor Wilde." He held out his hand. I did not take it.

He glanced down at his tablet. "I see. Holland is your name. All right then." He read a little more and tapped the screen.

He set the tablet aside, and looked at me. "I understand this is a delicate situation. Depending upon the outcome, there are various ways to proceed. All right?"

My head spun. Delicate? Had Orion told him about us, about the fake claim? I couldn't think. "All right," I replied.

"Normally, I have nurses who do this sort of thing. But for Orion, I'm seeing to this personally. Can you roll up your sleeve for me?"

With a quick glance at Orion, who looked on with a calm I was suddenly thankful for, I pulled up my sleeve.

Quickly, the doctor wrapped a tourniquet around my upper arm, tapped the inside of my elbow and turned away. "Perfect," he said.

Before I knew it, he'd stuck in a needle and the vial of blood was drawn out in seconds. He set it aside and took off the tourniquet, then deftly opened a small package of gauze, laid it over the needle prick, and taped it to me.

"And we're done," he said, a little too jolly.

I never felt any pain.

"I'll see you both tomorrow at this same time for the results, then, all right?"

"Yes." Orion said, and stood as I slid off the table.

"Will you personally be bringing more Omega patients to me from your farm?" Doctor Wilde asked. There was much innuendo in that question. But it told me that maybe Orion had not divulged all of our secrets to him.

"No. Orion lives with me now. He will be your patient, but Zilly's has its own connections to another hospital and their own Alpha doctors," Orion explained.

Doctor Wilde raised an eyebrow. "I see." He glanced again at me.

Orion said nothing more, not explaining what I was to him, or why I was the only one getting special, personalized treatment under his authority.

Once back in the limo, Orion glanced at me. "Are you all right?"

The limo pulled out of the parking garage and onto the busy street. "It doesn't hurt if that's what you mean."

He shook his head.

"You didn't tell him our secret, did you?"

"No. But obviously he could guess I am making a claim. He doesn't know anything else."

"Good." But I couldn't help but frown. "But waiting for the results, well, I won't be getting any sleep again tonight."

He said, "I'll take you somewhere nice. We'll order a bottle of wine for each of us."

"Will that help?" I didn't mean my words to come out clipped.

"It will."

He was so nice to me I almost couldn't stand it. Almost. There was something between us. But I couldn't see that far ahead right now. I couldn't allow myself to acknowledge it.

In my broken soul, thinking about having real feelings for an Alpha felt far too devastating. But on his word, I let him console my nerves with a good meal. And at dinner, I did drink the entire bottle of wine.

I practically wobbled into the house. It was past dark when we arrived home and Snowball greeted us in the foyer with his arched, dark silhouette as if to reprimand us for being gone too long.

I reached down to pet him, my head swimming, my balance off, and he purred. I nearly fell over.

Orion caught me.

I turned and grabbed onto his shoulders. He looked so well put together, so in control—and he smelled good, like rain spiced with cinnamon and warm, so warm. In my drunken moment, I didn't think of him as an Alpha, but just someone safe. Someone who was making all my problems go away.

I didn't want pity or charity, but this felt different, like he wanted to help me pull myself together, not do it all for me. It was why he'd given me a job. He was helping me be whole again.

But why did I have to be drunk to realize it?

My forehead came up to his jaw and pressed there against the hard bone and slight scruff. I moved to rub my skin against that and my whole body flared with warmth.

He had his hands under my arms to balance me and I felt him push a little, trying to right me.

I bowed my head into his neck and breathed in. Serene and fresh. A power combined with a nature to stop and listen even to the rudest critics of his farm who yelled at owners because they had nothing to lose after nearly dying. Me. He'd stopped everything. He'd turned. He'd listened. To me.

I breathed deeply of it all. "Orion, you have to—" I gulped. "Please—"

His hands gripped firmer, pushing me back so I couldn't nuzzle. "Coffee?" he softly asked. "Or do you need to lie down imminently?"

"What?"

"You're drunk. You need to lie down, I think," he said. "Yes."

He set me back a little more but kept one hand under my arm to help me walk without falling.

The staircase loomed up and up, never ending. The cat followed us on silent paws.

The next thing I knew, I was in my room with the blue walls and the dark, soft spread. He helped me sit and lie back, and he removed my shoes. What was happening was out of my control. I wanted something so far away, so distant I felt like crying. It was out of my reach. It was in my heart but buried deep. It was a need that required a trust I would never have.

I turned my head into the pillow so Orion couldn't see any of my thoughts displayed on my face. I said in my voice that sounded far away, "You can go."

"Not until I see that you're okay."

I peered at him with one eye and watched him bring a trash can and place it beside the bed.

"What's that for?"

"In case you feel sick."

"Oh."

He pulled the comforter from the foot of the bed over my still-clothed legs.

"There's water on the nightstand," he said.

"That's good," I mumbled.

"The phone I gave you is on the nightstand, too. Call me if you need me."

"You can go." I squirmed deeper into the blankets and pillows as I saw him move to the foot of the bed. Panic shot through me. "No! Don't go!"

"I won't."

After that, I don't know how long he stayed. I felt Snowball jump up onto the bed and settle himself against my legs. I strayed in and out of weird sleep that felt hot and cold.

I wanted him there. I liked knowing he stood by close but not too close. But I didn't want to like it.

I had no experience. I was too young for all of this. Everything that had happened and was happening seemed like a dream.

But it was no dream. And all my problems were not going to vanish by morning.

Chapter Fourteen

Orion

I stayed away from my office all morning and sat in the dining room waiting for Holland to come down. He did. Eventually.

Freshly showered, he had on clean clothes, though they were still his Zilly's uniform of black trousers and white shirt. I still hadn't seen him wearing the jeans I'd given the Omegas at Zilly's.

I'd ordered new clothes for him the day I brought him home, and instructed him to browse for more, but there hadn't been time for them to arrive. I figured we'd shop for all the more personal things he might want later.

When he entered the room, I looked up and our gazes met. As usual, his strength came through his stance, keeping himself steady, eyes locked. The only indication he might have retained some residual embarrassment from last night was an edge of pink flush at the tops of his cheeks. He looked well-rested and fearless.

Was this the same boy who'd nuzzled me and said "Don't go" last night?

"It's past breakfast," he said. "What are you still doing in here?"

"Reading," I replied, holding up my tablet. My dishes from breakfast had long since been cleared, but I had a fresh pot of coffee.

"Oh."

He got some food and came to sit in his usual space at the head of the table. His scent washed over me, soapy clean with a hint of flowers. All Omegas smelled good to all Alphas, but some had that special extra something that could not be defined that made an Alpha take a second look.

Holland had that for me from day one.

"Is there a plan for today?" Holland asked, using his knife to butter some cold toast.

"Other than our appointment at four, no."

"Hmm. What if I don't want to go today?"

"What?"

"What I if I don't want to know the results?"

I didn't understand why he wouldn't want to know. But as I thought about it, the next second I did understand.

"We can cancel."

To be reminded over and over of what Bosk did to him had to be a level of Hell all to itself. I wanted to be there for him. I wanted to be his friend. But I didn't know if he'd let me. Not without a bottle of wine in him first, and then, well, that wasn't real. That wasn't Holland being his true self.

"Do you want me to cancel the appointment, then?" I asked when he didn't reply.

He chewed, staring at his plate, then took another bite of his eggs. Without looking up, he finally said, "I guess not."

His hair took on the shadowy tones of the room and the darkening light outside from an overcast day. Deep shades of black on black strands scattered across his forehead and right cheek.

Yesterday had been clear, but today a storm brewed. Weather reports said it was coming from the west.

Stormy. His hair looked stormy.

"Did Snowball sleep with you all night?" I asked, changing the subject.

"I guess. He was on my bed when I got up."

"He likes you."

He did not reply.

When Holland finished eating, he stood. "I'm going to find that pool of yours. I'd like to sit out for a while."

A pool patio was technically where we'd first met.

"There are blankets in the hall closet by the patio entrance if you get cold," I called just as he turned out the door.

I heard his footsteps retreat. It was as if I'd had a conversation with a ghost.

I wanted to check on him all afternoon but held myself back. He never came to the dining room for a late lunch, but by three-thirty, as I descended the staircase toward the front door, I saw him waiting in the foyer with Alston hovering nervously nearby, trying not to look at him.

A light rain pattered against the sides of the house.

Holland had no coat. I went to a front closet where I kept coats and scarves and pulled out one of my jackets and brought it to him.

"It will be a little big on you, I think, but keep you warm."

He took it and shrugged into it. It dwarfed him. The arms were far too long and hid his hands. The hem hung to his knees. But the black color looked good on him.

Alston handed me a large umbrella, and we went out into the rain.

The limo was waiting.

We got inside with only a few raindrops splashing onto the leather couches. Once seated, the driver took off. I could hear the water rolling against the tires, a sort of sleepy, lonely sound… like a distant sea.

I brought out two beers.

"I think I had enough to drink last night," Holland said.

I set it on the drink stand next to him anyway.

The entire drive, he barely moved. He had his head turned, staring out the rain spattered window, his profile defiant, immovable. I admired him for being who he was. But he didn't know that and if I told him he wouldn't have believed it.

The tension in the air seemed to zap like static despite the one hundred percent humidity.

I wanted—what did I want to do? Take him by the hand or the arm, or around the waist. Sweep him away, far away, where no one knew him or us. Where we were strangers starting over, where I could meet him on a level of

128

no fear, and where maybe his storm-blue eyes might know calm even if only for short periods of time.

The limo entered the city, which was gray and half covered in fog. When we reached the dark parking garage with its yellow sodium lights, it had felt like the drive had gone on far too long, and yet it also felt as if no time had passed.

Holland showed no sign of nervousness when exiting the car.

My own heart vibrated high in my chest.

Approaching the elevator, I wanted to take his hand. What was wrong with me?

He entered the elevator first. I pushed the button for the seventeenth floor.

There, Doctor Wilde's pretty Omega husband from yesterday met us and ushered us immediately into the same room where he had drawn Holland's blood.

I glanced at my phone about every minute we waited, which was how I knew we'd waited five whole minutes in utter silence. It seemed longer.

Finally, the door opened.

Doctor Wilde stepped in, glancing at both of us and holding out his hand to mine in greeting. When he tried to shake Holland's hand, of course Holland turned away.

"I have your results."

"That's why we came," Holland said, voice empty, face hard.

"Yes. It's a matter of some delicacy, and I can see why you're both looking a bit tense."

I wanted to yell at him. *Get on with it! Just tell us!*

Holland and I stood side by side. We had not bothered to utilize the two chairs, or the exam table. We were simply waiting for words the doctor would not communicate any other way but in person.

Doctor Wilde leaned against the clean, white counter. He held a paper file in his hands.

"It's not as straight-forward as it could be, I'm afraid," he began.

"What's that supposed to mean?" Holland's words shot from his mouth with barely disguised fury.

"Your blood results show a mate-bond, but it's faint. Not strong at all. Is your mate, by any chance, deceased?"

All the blood seemed to drain from Holland's face.

I put out a hand to his lower back, not quite touching, but there in case he needed my support.

Holland let out a stifled grunt.

I said, "No. He's not deceased. The bond may have been formed when he was in an altered state and Holland was unconscious."

Blunt, the doctor asked, "It was forced?"

It wasn't my place to answer. I glanced at Holland.

Holland opened his mouth. "I did not consent." His chin moved forward and back as he clenched and unclenched his jaw.

As if he were lecturing a room full of students, the doctor began. "The properties in the blood that show a mate-bond reflect chemical changes in the body and brain. These are present in the sample, but diluted. That's why I wondered if the Alpha was dead. We see that when mate-bonded pairs lose a mate. But if he is alive, then where is he? Why is he not here with you?"

I bristled at the question. Holland had already answered. "He told you," I said. "He didn't consent."

"It is very difficult if not impossible to form a bond by rape. Did he knot you?"

The question horrified me.

Holland's face went even paler.

"He told you he was unconscious. How would he know?"

For my whole life, Doctor Wilde had seen me. He'd been gentle and kind. But right now, I didn't like him one bit. He seemed unconcerned that Holland had been raped, or that even now he suffered.

"It is a fact that sometimes my patients lie. I'm not saying this is the case here—"

"How do I undo it!" Holland's clipped voice interrupted, and he actually took a sudden half-step toward the doctor.

"Undo? But the mate-bond is sacred."

Holland faced him now, and I saw his eyes flash. "This is not sacred!" His lips curled.

Doctor Wilde looked at me as if I should control my Omega. But he wasn't mine to control. I might want Holland as mine, but I had no fantasies of ever controlling him. I liked that he was bold and strong and challenging. If I tried to subdue him, or diminish his anger, what would that make me? Why would I want to destroy that very fire in him that made him into more than a survivor, but a human who deserved respect?

I met Doctor Wilde's eyes and took a half-step back.

"These are things not talked about or widely shared, especially with Omegas," Wilde said.

"You will tell me." Holland's fists pressed against the outsides of his thighs.

Wilde glanced again at me.

I raised my eyebrows and smirked.

Holland spoke again. "I tried to look it all up on the Internet. There's no information. It's censored. Why the secrets? Even from other Alphas?"

"Because there really are no real scientific ways to dissolve bonds. Not really. It's just not done. The bond is more mystical than anything-- it's not scientific in the sense that you can take a pill and have the bond removed."

"What does that mean?" Holland was relentless. "Don't couples get divorced?"

"It's rare but it happens. Usually they find another to bond to. That second bonding will always dissolve the first. There are rare cases where two Omegas can be bonded at once to one Alpha. But two Alphas cannot claim the same Omega. Not that I've ever heard of."

"So you're saying I must bond with someone else to dissolve this current bond?"

Wilde nodded. "It wouldn't be difficult since this is weak. The factors that lead to a bond are, as I said, diminished in your blood, meaning they are still new, not fully formed. But they will form over time if you do nothing. They will get stronger. And you will feel a call to him, especially if he enters the Burn."

Holland's mouth fell open. Air came out in a rush. He looked like he might be sick. "It's been more than seven months. I never felt any call. Don't Alphas have a Burn about every two months?"

Wilde nodded. "That's true. But you said your mate was in an altered state. If he's on medication, or mentally ill, or both, he might not feel the Burn at all. Or maybe once a year. It can vary."

Holland looked horrified. "You said there were ways. Plural. Is there any other way to dissolve the bond?"

"Well, in old times there was the Challenge."

"You're kidding!" I couldn't keep my mouth shut now. "I've only ever heard of that in history texts. That hasn't been legal in hundreds of years."

Wilde shrugged.

"What's the Challenge?" Holland asked, still far too pale, his fists banging against his legs.

"Didn't your history texts teach you this?" Wilde asked.

"He grew up on a chattel farm," I said quickly.

"Ah yes, Zilly's. Of course I knew that." Wilde stared for a few seconds at Holland as if he were an insect. He said, "In the past, the Challenge was made with or without a bond. Two Alphas make a claim on the same Omega. Or an Alpha makes a claim on an already bonded Omega. The Alphas fight. To the death."

"You state that as if it still goes on. It's illegal. An Alpha killing another Alpha is murder," I said.

Wilde nodded. "It is illegal in this country. But a few countries still practice it. Shrouded in rites and secrecy. Antiquity. Odd ritual. Religion. It's not spoken of. It's not recorded. You won't find mention on the Internet except in historical texts."

"Are those the only ways to break the bond?" Holland asked. His breath rushed past his lips.

Wilde turned from Holland to me. "That's all I have. I'm sorry if the news is bad."

"If? He told us he did not consent. It's terrible news." I opened the door, not waiting for Wilde to do it. "We'll see our way out."

"Orion," Wilde called.

I did not turn.

"I wish I had better news," he finished.

I didn't reply.

Holland preceded me down the hall to the elevator.

On our way down to the parking garage, neither of us looked at the other.

My driver bowed to us and opened the doors to the limo.

As the doors closed behind us, and the car began to move, I started to speak. "Holland--"

"I don't want to talk right now," he interrupted. But while his voice had been full of sharp inflections to Wilde, he'd softened it somewhat with me.

I leaned back and endured the drive home.

The limo let us out at the front path that led to the porch. I got out first. Holland was behind me. A little too close.

He pushed past me, hand on my back, nearly knocking me aside and tripping over the bottom of the door.

The side yard was filled with bushes but there were spaces between them. He ran past them and onto the grassy slope that led toward the back. The estate went on for many more acres back there, a trimmed and well-manicured landscape of jacarandas and willows, pine and eucalyptus.

The field was still damp from rain, smelling of wet earth and leaves. He half slid as he ran, almost falling again, his shoes shining with moisture.

He rounded the far end of the house, headed for the pool area, just as I started to go after him.

My driver, wisely, turned away and did not interfere.

I caught up to Holland easily once he had made it out back and slowed. I came up to him fast, and touched him on the elbow.

Holland turned in a dash of fury, hands out. His face was turned in, eyes wild as they looked past me, mouth scrunched down hard. His eyebrows were so close together they looked like one line.

"I'm bonded to a monster. A monster!" His voice came from some hollow place inside him, full of echoes and cries. Seething, frenzied, and very very lost.

I wanted to hold him but he would never allow that.

"There's nothing we can do!" he yelled.

I stood before him and rage leaped within me as well. I cared about him. Too much. Softly, I said, "I could kill him."

I already felt it—the propriety over Holland. It occupied my thoughts day and night. Holland was mine. I claimed him. Even if it was fake to him, it had become real to me.

So what if the Challenge only happened in the old days or in some secret sect in a foreign country. I'd break the law to engage it. I'd break all laws for Holland. I'd known it for some time now, even in the early days of our emails.

Even if Holland had never heard of the Challenge, I had. I'd learned it in the history texts my tutors had made me read. Wilde had described it only briefly. Centuries ago, two Alphas who made a claim on the same Omega would face the Challenge. My text books had funky illustrations. Fancy arenas. Full moon gatherings. Witnesses standing around in robes like it was a graduation or a birthday.

After much feasting and drinking, the two Alphas would face off in the stone-floored arena and fight to the death. Maybe one was in the Burn. Maybe they both were. It would be bloody. Some of my text books showed them fighting naked and erect, like mindless animals in rut, sometimes even using their cocks as weapons, trying to rape each other right at the onset of a kill. It was disgusting and feral. A tradition best left to the distant past.

But even that—

A feeling that I wanted even that, that I might kill for Holland, rose up in me. It was like nothing I'd ever felt before. I didn't have a bond with him, and only a fake claim. Yet it felt real.

But it couldn't be real; it had to be the result of my own outrage for him. For his predicament. For the horror he'd lived through.

"Why didn't my scent change? Why can't I feel it?"

Intermittent drops of rain fell around us. The pool flickered off to our right, and I could see the droplets making little circles in the water's surface. Everything smelled of water and tears and desperation. Like drowning.

"I don't know," I said, as Holland's new plea broke my reverie.

"If the bond is real, wouldn't it be noticed? A change in my scent?"

"The trauma. That has to be why." A damp gust of wind whipped over me, sweeping my hair into my face and I raised my hand to push it back. My fingers tangled in it, yanking it hard. The pain made me gasp. "Ah! This is so frustrating!"

"For me, not you!"

"For me, too! Holland, damn it, don't you know by now, after these months? I don't care if it was only emails where we communicated. I think I'm quite obvious. Or you're just unobservant if you can't see it. I'd do anything for you!"

There. The truth. It was out now.

He stared up at me, blue eyes unreadable. Chest heaving.

"I would do anything to keep you safe, including things you don't want." More truth. Too much? I'd said it now and there was no turning back.

I watched him, his eyes boring into me. But this time, it was he who dropped his gaze first. He who stood before me. He kicked at the wet grass and his shoes shone with rain. My coat on him hung long, making him look even more bedraggled than he was.

Finally, he looked up at me again, blinking hard. "What do you even see when you look at me?"

I must not have answered fast enough, because he turned away, grumbling, "I thought so!"

"Wait!" I reached out for him. This time my hand brushed against his upper arm. "You didn't give me time to answer. What do I see when I look at you?"

He did not pull away from my touch, but he didn't turn back to face me, either. He appeared to be listening.

Without waiting another second, I said, "I see you. Just you. Not your name, not your status. Just a man who is brilliant, brave, daring and a survivor. You fling challenges everywhere you go. That's a good thing. That's a start to patching up such a broken world. You're someone who sees the world differently and isn't afraid to say. That's what I see, and it's what I saw when we first met. I admire it greatly."

Voice low, "You think we're friends."

"I was hoping."

When he finally faced me, his chin was up, his eyes open, but the deep blue of them had darkened. Like the sky around us. Voice steady and strong, he said, "You won't let Bosk take me."

I pressed my lips tight and shook my head.

He took a step forward. My hand pressed harder against his arm before I let it fall.

"Promise me," he said.

"I promise with everything I am, everything I can give."

Holland clasped his hands together, the sleeves of my coat which was too big for him falling back. He put his clasped hands to his chest, holding them there as if he were cold.

"Friends," he said. He took a deep breath and started walking back toward the front of the house.

It was a positive step at least. Something we could work with.

I sighed and followed him inside.

Chapter Fifteen

Holland

The coat was bulky. I hated the weight of it on my skin. But it smelled like Orion, like coffee and cinnamon and summer sun.

The wind blew sprays of water in my face from the trees overhead.

We walked back to the front path and the porch, Orion, oddly, a step behind me.

A still-angry voice deep in my head said, *Fuck, you have a pet Alpha now.*

But I didn't really think of Orion in that way. Harly would say I had issues. And he'd be right.

It had been only months that I'd known him. And two nights I'd spent living in his house. It was nothing in the huge span of time. But he'd already made more promises to me than anyone I'd ever known.

I might have brushed it off to simple, out of control attraction. But Orion was in control. Orion was not an erratic Alpha and if I told him to back off, he backed off.

He was really a nice guy, I had to admit. He deserved better than me.

When we got inside, Orion's Alpha butler Alston took our coats away, probably to be washed and dried and buffed to perfection. My clothes had stayed dry, but my shoes were wet.

As I was about to take them off, thinking I might place them by the front door, another servant came in to the foyer.

"Shoes, sir?" He spoke directly to Orion.

Orion and I both bent to remove them.

Now in our stocking feet, we stood, both of us slightly shivering.

"Let's go into the dining room for an early dinner. There's a fire place in there. I'll have Alston light it."

"Can we have wine?" My question came out more sour than I intended.

"I was thinking of breaking out the harder stuff."

"What's that?"

"Whiskey. You'll love it."

"All right."

This time Orion led the way.

I hadn't had any lunch. My nerves had strung me up inside and out and I hadn't been hungry. But now that I knew about my blood test, even though the news was bad, I realized I was hungry now, and tired and aching, and I just wanted to sit, eat and get warm.

Orion was texting as he entered the dining room. Immediately, Alston showed up and started a fire.

In a sort of alcove where the dining area curved away, there was a couch near the hearth, with a low table.

Orion brought square, shallow glasses and a clear decanter of brown liquid. He poured a small amount in each glass, handed one to me, and sat on the couch beside me.

I sniffed the concoction within the strange glass. It was sharp and my eyes watered for a second until I blinked them clear.

Orion swirled his drink in his glass once before upending it and gulping it all down. He poured himself another inch or so of the liquid and stared at it.

I swirled my glass. It splashed a bit. Then I put the rim of the glass to my lips and took a sip.

All the way down it warmed me. The aftertaste was hot, almost like a burn, almost like the way tree sap smelled on a hot day. I could not describe it any other way.

Orion looked at me. "Well?"

"Interesting," I replied, before taking another sip.

We sat and drank, silent and watching the flames. I heard footfalls and plates and cutlery jingling behind me as the Alpha servants brought in dishes to the buffet for us to help ourselves.

The couch was soft and cushioned my weight perfectly. The day had been hard.

I didn't want to move. But I didn't want to avoid what must be talked about.

"Bosk could go into the Burn at any time," I blurted out. "Your fake bond-mate claim won't work, though I appreciate you trying. But I do not intend to go to him. Ever."

Orion nodded, staring into his drink.

"I don't know what that might feel like if he does go into the Burn, and I don't ever want to know," I added. "But what if the urge is too strong?"

"You've never talked about this feeling with other bonded Omegas?"

"I've never known any bonded Omegas. The mated ones always leave. I have read about it, though. The pull to your mate is magnetic. You want to be with him during his Burn to the exclusion of all else. But how could that be? My hatred for Bosk is not going to simply vanish."

I couldn't believe I was having this conversation with another Alpha. But I trusted Orion. I felt like a fool, but I knew I was also lucky. If I'd never met Orion, I'd be facing all this alone at the farm, or in an institution, with no recourse.

I felt sick.

I told myself there was no way I would allow Bosk to intrude on my thoughts that way, to invade me with his Burn and the disgusting urge to go to him against my will. But would I ever have that sort of control?

"You have to do it tonight."

Orion turned and stared at me. "What?"

My cheeks flamed. The idea of Orion having me was far from disgusting, and if I weren't so broken I might have actively wanted it. "We're friends, you said. All right, then. You have to do whatever you can to break this bond inside me."

"You mean kill him?"

Stunned, I met his eyes. Only Orion would not jump to conclusions. I started to laugh, though nothing was funny. None of it. My chest ached.

"I have no doubt if we were three hundred years in the past you would Challenge for me. But no, that isn't what I meant."

I could barely get the words out. My laughter took over again, bending me over, cramping my stomach.

Orion put his hand on my back and slowly pressed. All the warmth of the hearth and the room seemed to focus on that hand where it touched me mid-spine, a golden edged heat coming into me, steadying, gentle, like a promise from childhood coming back to me that I'd forgotten I'd made to myself.

"You realize it isn't just about the, um, sex," he said.

How cute; he was being shy with me.

"It has to happen during a Burn," he said gently.

How could I have forgotten that?

"When is your next Burn?" I sounded like an insolent child. Bratty. Angry.

"Next month."

Did we even have that much time?

I leaned forward, elbows on my knees, and put my chin against my clasped hands. I stared into the battling flames in front of me until my eyes ached.

"This isn't going to work, then, is it?" I said. I wasn't going to dance around this subject. We needed everything out on the table.

"Holland," he said softly.

The hair on my nape stood up, but not creepy. It was a soft and insistent tingle.

"A real bond is more than just—just sex. It's a relationship, too," he said softly.

"Tell that to--" I gulped. I wasn't going to say his name out loud. "Him."

"It's not a real bond. Not solid."

"Doctor Wilde didn't seem to think so. He said it would grow stronger with time. It would take over."

Holland's hand moved on my back very gently. He said, "I heard him. But he isn't seeing this from your point of view. Everyone is different. Unique. And this is a very personal matter. To you. About you. He wouldn't talk about things like Omegas fighting mate-bonds because it doesn't matter to him. He's an Alpha, and a happily bonded one. It doesn't concern him."

"He's a doctor. You'd think he'd have seen it all."

"He probably has, but that doesn't mean he can fix the problems. He does diagnoses. And he prescribes. He's not a surgeon. And he's not a couples therapist."

I leaned back, turning to look at Orion again. His face was smooth and kind, his brown hair thick and rich, his dark eyes backlit with the flickering of the warm fire in the hearth.

It was in that moment I knew he'd been too amazing for me to comprehend. I couldn't allow it. I wouldn't let myself… to have such a friend in an Alpha, and a possible love. I'd built too many walls in the past months around any such thoughts.

But right now, I could see it all. How he'd worked hard to see me, the real me behind all the anger, and to help me.

I was too furious and hurt, too proud for help. But now I needed it. I needed it more than ever.

"You gave me that office at the farm when I barely knew you. Why?"

His eyebrows came together. A pained smile crossed his eyes, gentling in a slight curve at his lips. I saw he couldn't speak.

I unclasped my hands and leaned into him, letting his essence come into my lungs, the slight soap-scent of his aftershave, the emanating sweetness.

"Is it because you wanted to be friends?" I asked.

He did not reply. But I saw it in his face, how he looked at me, how his throat moved as he swallowed against words he would not say probably for fear that I'd run.

I would have run back then.

This man owned an Omega farm. This man was a spoiled and privileged rich guy from beyond my means. This man was too many times my hero for comfort.

And yet he had made promises. He had helped me. He had comforted me even if he didn't know he was doing it.

I narrowed the distance between us and pressed my mouth to his. It was to be a quick kiss. A brush. A meeting of lips.

His hand pressed against my back.

I didn't pull away and neither did he.

Seconds passed.

The room around us fled. Time and the world did not exist. Only this. Him. In front of me, the warmth of him, the safety. The caring.

My nose pushed against the side of his nose. Our chins bumped. Our foreheads brushed.

The tension inside me lifted to be replaced by a new tension simmering just under the skin. Yearning. The pressure like a hunger. A craving.

I had felt it that day by the pool at the farm when he'd walked up to the chain-link gate, when he'd spoken to me as if I were a normal person.

All Alphas since my attack reigned in my nightmares. But not him. Not Orion. My dreams of him had not been nightmares. And it made me angrier than ever.

But no longer was that anger directed toward him.

I lifted my hand between us and touched his chest. His heart was racing. His lungs heaved as he tried to catch his breath without pulling away from me.

My mouth opened to him just enough that I could take his breath to mine and mingle them.

Everything inside me surged up to a white hot core, like a sun trapped within. A star I'd thought had burned out.

My body tingled. My skin seemed to curl and coil. My cock—my damn cock got hard.

Finally, I had to pull back. My eyes were blurred. I saw only colors: brown hair, black shirt, the edges of the orange fire. My own arms clad in white.

"He can't have me," I whispered.

"He can't have you," Orion echoed. "I won't let him."

Was he as hard as I? Did he really want me, my broken soul?

Orion leaned toward the low table, letting my hand slide down his chest, and poured more whiskey into our two glasses. He took them both, handed me mine, and raised his to me.

I knew then we were going to spend the evening getting quietly drunk.

*

I woke in a patch of sun streaming in through a line where my curtains did not quite meet. The light rippled across the dark, shiny spread covering me.

I pushed it aside, seeing I was still dressed.

How had I gotten here?

Slowly, vague glimpses of memory returned. Orion. Square cut glasses. Whiskey and more whiskey.

And there had been a kiss, the most unbelievable kiss of two men drawn by different needs that merged into one need, one blazing ache.

I remembered getting up and moving around the mansion to different rooms, following Orion about, gasping at the hugeness, the openness of the house. And laughing. And draping myself over pinball machines in the game room as I tried to make the silver ball bearings go into the proper niches with my mind.

Damn, whiskey was good. Real good.

I remembered snatches of playing pool, and fucking it up so badly, tossing the balls into the pockets as if I were playing mini-basketball.

144

Orion's laugh. It was like a song, low and playing in my ears all around me.

I lay on the floor of the game room, cool marble against my cheek, chanting "more whiskey" and watched him play some game on a big wide screen. It was all color, no sense. Then I was lifted high, the room swirling about me. Then the stairs, as if I were floating up them. But strong arms encircled me, and strong legs propelled us up and up.

Next I knew, I was in my room and a man stood by my bedside just like the night before, removing my shoes, raising the coverlet over me, bending down and saying something soft and too sweet in my ear.

What was it?

I tried to remember. I could still feel his warm breath against my jaw and earlobe. A partial phrase. Some words. "…won't let…" "…mine…" "…forever…sweet…"

Now I sat up in the bed and my head began to pound. The room whirled a bit until I got my senses under control. I saw the trashcan by the bedside. Luckily, it was empty.

I managed to get up and walk to the bathroom. I thought I might throw up, but nothing happened. After a while, I turned on the shower to as hot as I could stand it, stripped and stepped in.

It was noon and by the time I got to the dining room, the buffet contained fruit, bread, cheese, ham, salami and other deli offerings.

Orion was nowhere in sight.

Alone, I made myself a plate of fruit and cheese, though my stomach soured at the thought of eating. I also made myself a coffee.

The fire was out in the hearth at the end of the room, the ash swept up as if nothing had ever occurred. I saw no sign of our whiskey bottle or our square glasses.

I sat down at a center seat of the long table and inhaled the steam from my coffee before finally deciding to take a sip. It felt wonderful going down, and after about two more sips, my stomach began to settle.

I heard a swish of cloth, the fall of a footstep. I turned to see Orion at the threshold of the entrance, his dark gaze falling over me like a warm, deep sunrise.

All I could think was: *I've felt those lips on mine. I've breathed his breath.*

My face warmed.

His mouth turned up. "You're awake."

"Am I?" I shot back. I rolled my eyes to take the sting out of my hard response.

He came forward, grabbing an apple from a nearby bowl of fruit, and sat beside me. It was stupid to sit like that, side by side. We couldn't easily see each other, if that was his intent. He should have gone to the chair across from mine. He should have—

What was I doing? Already criticizing him when he'd done nothing, really, when my quick assumption was he even wanted to see me, let alone speak to me?

His nearness to me affected me greatly. We sat, not touching, but our shoulders and thighs were too close. Too damn close.

I put a block of cheese in my mouth and chewed, not tasting it. But my stomach made a sound as I swallowed, as if rising up to grab the food it needed. It was pissed at missing dinner and being given only alcohol. It wanted to be appeased. And so did I.

I moved on my seat so I was angled toward Orion, who crunched on his apple like it was the only thing in the universe.

It wasn't. It wasn't and I wanted to tell him that.

"Hey," I said.

He glanced aside at me.

"I just wanted—" I frantically tried to think of what I wanted to say. "To, um, thank you for getting me to my room safe last night."

His eyes glimmered. "You're welcome."

"That's it?" I asked, unable to hide my disappointment. I mean, he had, like a puritan prince, carried me up the wide and palatial staircase to my opulent and exalted room next to his.

"What?" His eyes widened. His lips pressed tight as if suppressing a frown. Or a smile.

I could not suppress my own frown. No smile. *"That's it* is a common phrase meaning: Is there no more? It means is there no more than *you're welcome*?" I took a deep breath. Exasperated.

"Hmm."

That hum under his breath. It did so much to me.

I waited.

"Maybe I should have said: My pleasure."

I blinked twice. The light of the room nearly hurt. I wanted more shadows, more curtains, more comfort than light.

"Do we have to wait?" My voice came out scratchy.

"For what?"

"Until sunset? Dark? Bedtime?"

His mouth opened in surprise. "For?"

Fuck that. He wasn't dense, it was just that I'd trained him too well. My Alpha. I wasn't his pet. He was mine. And I'd trained him to fall back, stay away, not touch. At least, not much.

"We're going to break this bond, right? Do we have to wait to start the relationship? Is there some proper time?"

His eyebrows shot up. "No."

I leaned in much like last night. But this time I put my hand behind his neck and pulled him to me.

This time, when our lips touched we both seemed to sigh into each other, as if we'd been holding our breaths underwater for hours. In the same moment, our bodies scooted our chairs back. We stood; we embraced.

He leaned down and I opened my mouth to his and a long groan escaped me. Our tongues met and tasted, each to each. So deep. The intensity overriding any dizziness from last night's drink and this morning's hangover.

When I couldn't hold my breath any longer, I pulled back. "Take me upstairs," I demanded. It was unromantic the way I said it, but I really had no filter. Not these last months.

"Take you?"

"Pick me up," I demanded. *Again.* That word went unspoken. But the memory of how he'd carried me up those stairs wouldn't leave me. Like a game I wanted to play over and over.

I felt him turn and grip me, one hand snaking under my upper back, the other sliding along my thighs to the backs of my knees. He bent and before I could take another breath he had me up in his arms like I weighed nothing. Like I was his already.

Everything spun and I grabbed the shoulder seam of his blue, button-up shirt in a tight grip. As we strode out the door and down the hall, it was like flying.

I saw one Alpha servant, Alston perhaps, vanish around a corner and then we were gliding up, up. I could hear Orion's breaths close to my ear and his heart like a drum next to mine and feel the way his arms curved in gentle support, not too tight but tight enough. I knew I was something he would not let go of easily.

I bowed my head until my forehead touched the side of his face, my hair falling forward to curtain my eyes.

I didn't want to think about what I was doing, I just wanted to do it. Now. No thought. No fear. I wanted what I wanted, and that meant giving in, finally, to the surge in my veins, and the longing I never thought I'd feel.

"Orion, hurry," I heard myself say. Not words I would have thought might come from my mouth after only three nights in my new home.

"My room is closest."

"Your room, then," I breathed.

He pushed the door open with his body and practically slung me across the threshold. But he never faltered and I wrapped my other arm around his neck though I knew he'd surely die before dropping me.

148

His room was identical to mine, except it was done up in dark purples, lavenders and black.

On his bed, which was impeccably made, he gently lowered me, and our lips met again as he knelt over me, both hands cupping my face.

I easily pushed him until he rolled to the side and suddenly I was on top, an instinct. I didn't think twice about it, but I did notice how easily he went, how willing he was to lie back and let me lead. Had I been any other Omega, I might have found it odd.

But I wasn't any other Omega. I was me. Weird. Glib. Distracted, since I'd met him, by a fog I could not rise from.

My legs were between his as I pressed my chest to his, as I pushed up and over him to get better access to his mouth.

His hands rubbed up and down my back. Mine were on his shoulders, squeezing, and I trembled within as if a wind had formed inside me. New sensations began to roll through me.

Intellectually, I knew what to do. But what I wanted, and how the smoother nature of this might play out, I had less clue.

I moved my hands to Orion's wavy brown hair, weaving them through the tides of it, thick and soft, the beauty there for my exploration alone.

I knew arousal, but I'd never felt this before, how my skin flashed hot and cold in gentle waves, how the center of my stomach seemed to heat up until it melted my insides, everything liquid and yielding and hard at the same time.

I'd never felt myself this hard before, an ache longing for touch; my body was begging. My mind communicated to me in pure emotion. Nothing in the world mattered but this.

Orion was the one. Patient Orion. He wanted this, I knew, but he never would have started it. The closest touch he'd ever initiate was a look, a smile. Aside from emails and a private office on a farm where Omegas had few rights, all of which were initiations of a less personal sort, he had waited and never pushed.

Now I wanted him in far more than business. We had a fake contract, a fake claim. It wasn't enough. I needed him to break the bond within me to a monster. But I was also beyond all that.

How long had I been wanting him and denied any knowledge of that to myself? I'd coldly rationalized he was my type, and banned any further thought.

I had hated how I assumed he saw me. A victim. A pathetic Omega to save. But his words said he saw more.

I leaned down and his lips were like soft petals opening. I wasn't being saved by them, I was saving myself as I drank him, as I delved my tongue into his mouth.

It was lush to be with him like this, our mouths pressed tight. Pleasure rippled through me. Desires from dreams I forgot I'd ever had.

How many days had it been since I'd even touched myself? Half a year, at least.

The never-ending kiss lashed at my insides until I couldn't stand it, until I had to feel more. My hands moved from his face down to his chest, feeling for the buttons and the buttonholes in the cramped space between us.

Orion's hands pushed under my waistband, pulling my shirt up my back to my shoulders.

To properly undress, we had to separate.

I didn't like that at all because then I had time to look at him, and think too much. And wonder about all the wrong things. Like fear that this might not work out between us. And worry that my own body wasn't ready.

But I was ready. There was no denying my body thrilled to the touch of bare hands along my spine as Orion tried to get my shirt off. My own hands, fumbling at his throat and chest, couldn't accomplish their task fast enough.

I came up onto my knees, looking down at his deep, kind eyes, his gaze darkened by desire, his cheeks flushed. I wanted to feel him all over. I wanted to caress, rub, thrust.

I shrugged out of my shirt and draped it on the bedspread behind me.

150

Orion half sat up and did the same, tossing his shirt over the mattress edge.

The light in his room was bright through the half-open, fancy purple curtains. Daylight was invading our privacy, but I wanted to see him, every inch of him. Boldly, I began unbuckling his belt.

He gently inserted his hands beneath mine and took over undoing the clasp and the top button of his trousers.

I took the hint and undid my own trousers, pushing them down along with my underwear all the way, taking my socks with them as I kicked them out of sight.

Orion was still sliding his down when he looked up, eyes widening, at me poised before him, on my knees, breathing a little too roughly, my cock aching toward the ceiling. I went hot all over at his gaze, unsure for a moment, my personality demanding I not show it. I said curtly, "You're taking too long."

He blinked languidly, then slowly slid the cloth to his ankles, goading me, deliberately taking his time.

I didn't care because he revealed rippling muscles and long thighs and a thick cock that rose up, red at the tip and dusky dark all the way down to his balls.

I wasn't sure I would find him so beautiful after my last ordeal with an Alpha. But he was. More beautiful than my fantasies.

No thinking! I told myself. *Just feel. Just do.*

I leaned over him and gasped as our cocks touched, my hands going up over his hard stomach, feeling the wavelets of muscles there, then slowly up to his chest where the pecs, like rock, supported dark, erect nipples.

I lowered my head, my hair brushing his skin, and licked one. Just to taste. Just because it looked so needy.

He gasped and his hips jerked, our cocks bumping against one another.

I lowered my hips so my weight was on him, trapping our cocks between us, and licked again.

"Holland."

"Let me," I whispered.

"Yes."

"Stay still while I—"

"I won't move," he interrupted breathlessly.

He remained true to his word and allowed me every touch I wanted, every infraction I could think of, but wholly welcomed, consenting.

I ran my hands over his chest and arms.

I licked by his shoulder where the softest flesh of the upper arm ended, tasting only sweetness. I nuzzled his neck, his sides. I circled his bellybutton with my tongue.

I pulled back and let the air instead of my own body surround that beautiful cock. It jutted up tall and strong, thick at the base, rounded and plump at the tip, and too lovely to describe beyond that.

I pushed his thighs apart more and he let me, moving them where I wanted, bending his knees to make it easier. I ran my fingers over his balls and further behind, petting, rubbing at the cleft of his buttocks, the heat there alive and tight.

His hips were lean. I wanted him to lie back and spread further. It was like at the farm when I'd suddenly had no filters, but that was for speech and anger. Now those filters vanished in the light of what I wanted. More of him. More.

I ran my palms, face up, under his ass and kneaded. And spread him.

He'd been making little groans but now he moaned aloud.

I let one forefinger travel to his entrance and push in less than half an inch.

He moaned so loud I thought at first I'd hurt him.

I snatched my hand away. Was this wrong? He was the Alpha. He probably wouldn't want it.

"Don't stop." His voice rang with neediness, a low and unexpected whine.

"You like it? Don't most Alphas want..?" I stopped, unsure.

152

"I'm not most Alphas." He sounded almost drunk. "It's why I—I don't use the chattel farms. The Omegas are so rigidly taught." He expelled a breath as if embarrassed.

I was taught on a farm. But all that went out the window right now as I gave in to what I wanted. How I saw him and the ways I wanted to explore that felt like the real me.

Orion seemed willing to go right along with me.

I put my finger back and dry-entered again. It seemed forced, but he moaned again.

I was inexperienced, but not uneducated. "Is there lube anywhere in this room?"

"Yes," he said, and I lifted my head to see him start to laugh, his face pained, his eyes almost all the way shut.

His fists punched the bed and he sat up.

"Where?"

"Top drawer by the bed." He motioned with his hand.

As I leaned toward the night table, I saw him look me up and down, and I would have backed away if it had seemed anything like before, out of control or wrong or dirty, but nothing was out of control, or seemed dirty or lascivious. He was only kind and adoring, and he said, "You're so beautiful."

I couldn't think of a response, so I rushed to open the drawer, my cock bobbing between my legs as I shifted my weight, and found the shiny, brand new bottle. I gripped its coldness in my palm.

I showed it to him.

"Use it," he said, his head turning on the pillows, his knees bending and spreading to make room for me to re-settle between them.

It seemed so easy. He wanted this, and I wanted to touch, so I poured some lube into my hand and onto my fingers and ran them up and down his crack.

His cock twitched.

It was lovely. Amazing. On sudden impulse, I leaned down and ran my tongue all over the tip of his erection.

He let out a yell, but remained still as I pushed my finger inside him, deeper this time with the lube helping to ease the way, and at the same time I sucked the head of his cock into my mouth.

My own cock throbbed to do this. I didn't think it would turn me on so much, but everything was just right for me. I wanted him. It didn't seem wrong. It seemed very very right as he moved his hips slightly to take more of my finger into him and push more of his cock into my mouth.

Had he been penetrated before?

He started to writhe and groan and I sucked hard while I put a second finger into him.

My whole body shivered and trembled in need as I did this, not because I wanted to be where he was, no, not on my back, not yet, but because I wanted to do this to him. For him.

I moved my fingers in and out of him. He quivered and opened more.

I tasted his essence, like tart salt, on the edge of my tongue as he grew more wet and aroused at the tip of his cock, which hardened even more in my mouth, jutting toward the back, making me swallow.

"Ah!" He yelled and a hand caught my shoulder, gently pushing. "I'll come," he said softly. "Too fast. I want you to put yourself inside me."

I pulled off his cock and it fell hard and wet to his belly. "You've done this before," I accused.

He closed his eyes, giving a single nod.

"But you're an Alpha."

"Some Alphas like it. Please, I like it."

I gulped. He was the boss. The owner of Zilly's. A big and beautiful Alpha. And he wanted this.

I had wanted it from the moment I'd touched him there, between his cheeks, watching as he responded, as his muscles tightened and sucked my fingers into him. My cock throbbed to be where my fingers had been, and I could have come from just the thought of his body encasing my hardness.

I couldn't believe how quickly, how thoroughly I'd desired this, as if I were the one soon to be out of control. I never knew. I had not allowed myself to think of sex with an Alpha in this way.

"Do you want to?" he asked.

I nodded, clearing my throat. Fuck. It was more than want. Quickly, I grabbed up the bottle of lube and poured some onto my cock, trying not to touch myself for fear I'd come before I could get what I really wanted. Inside him. Inside that sweet grip I'd felt on my fingers.

My cock glistened as he pulled his legs up fast.

"Do it, just do it," he said hoarsely.

I pushed my cock against the crack of his ass, rubbing the head all along it.

He reached around his thighs and pulled his cheeks wider. I saw him open for me, the dark entrance oiled and ready, and it didn't even register that it might be difficult, as I'd been taught it could be.

I moved until the head of my cock was right there, at the aperture which seemed to already be sucking at the tip, and lightly pushed. The head of my cock slid against it and he opened more—such control—and as I gave only a bit more pressure, he moved his hips and took me, gliding, into him, all heat and oil and tightness surrounding me.

Air rushed from my lungs. It felt so good. Beyond my imaginings. Feeling bolder, and even more unfiltered, I pushed harder and slid all the way to the base of my cock.

"Fuck!"

I was flushed and almost embarrassed, except I was too busy feeling so euphoric that I opened my mouth and confessed. "That's fucking amazing!"

A groan and a chuckle escaped him.

I could be myself in this moment, unfettered by laws and rules and learned behaviors, and I leaned over him in a surge of utter gratitude.

"Okay?" I asked.

"So much better than okay. Move now," he instructed.

I stared at his fluttered eyelids, body ready but my mind still wondering. Was it too fast? Too much?

"Damn you, move!" He gripped my shoulders, pulled me down to him and kissed me.

I pulled back and out of him most of the way as he groaned into my mouth. Then I thrust. And thrust again.

His arms wrapped around me, and his thighs squeezed against my hips.

Tight, everything was so tight, and I heard him say against my mouth, "Faster now."

I pumped my hips and the ecstasy rolled over me. I wasn't going to last. My first time, well, who cared if I made it last? All that mattered was becoming lost in pure sensation, and feeling safe doing so. This couldn't be the only time I'd ever feel like this. I wouldn't allow it. With Orion, I wanted more days, more nights, my bed, his bed. I could already tell I would not be satisfied with one time.

Never in a million years would I have thought it could be like this. It didn't produce children, so it wasn't taught. Not this. Not anything but submission for Omegas.

He kissed me harder, then turned to mouth my cheek and said, "It's so good. I love it. I can't hold on, I'm going to--"

"Let it," I whispered back, and as I tried to squeeze my hand between us, I felt him hard and throbbing, then pulsing, and the hot dampness spread between us as my fingers curled around his length and stroked him through his climax.

It was too much as his muscles tightened around my cock. But the lube allowed me two more smooth thrusts before I couldn't hold back, before everything around me erupted in a beautiful blue-white light.

A voice filled with cries swelled about us—mine or his, I couldn't tell.

He pulled me down to him and kissed me over and over, our mouths merging, our bodies slick and hard and clinging. I knew it would end, but wished with all my heart for it to keep on going, just me and him, forever until nothing else existed, until we were all that was or ever would be.

His hands went up and down my back, then cupped my buttocks and pulled me closer, his palms pressing in, stroking, rubbing so gently, so beautifully.

I was still in him when I'd stopped coming. His own cock, trapped between us, throbbed and throbbed and I wondered if he'd come so hard he'd formed a knot. Alphas could knot without the Burn, but not all that often from what I'd read. It took great need, great energy, great passion.

I wanted to lift up and see, but he held me tight and our bodies rippled in afterglow. Maybe he was still coming. Maybe he didn't know, either, so I stayed still and kissed him hard, my hands raking through his damp and tired curls.

Finally, I pulled away and put my cheek against his chest, listening to his heart thrum in tune with his cock throbbing against my belly.

I closed my eyes and felt myself float along with that rhythm. When I opened them again, I realized I'd dozed off.

Mortified, I lifted my head, but felt Orion's arms tighten as his body shifted. He gave a low moan and turned us both until we were on our sides facing each other.

Sometime during my brief sleep, my cock had softened and slipped from his body.

But still, every part of me was sensitive, tingly, turned on.

Orion brushed his lips to mine and pulled away, saying softly. "I'll be right back."

I closed my eyes, listening to his feet pad across the rug and tile. The bathroom door closed and I heard water rushing.

I opened my eyes and the brightness from the half-curtained window made me wince as I ran my hand down my sticky body. I needed a shower, too.

I didn't want to get up. The top cover was over me up to my waist. Orion must've brought it up while I slept. A gentleman through and through.

After a moment, I slid off the bed and went to the bathroom door. It was ajar and I pushed it open.

I heard the shower before I looked around the corner to see Orion standing behind the glass door, his hands pushing back his thick, wet hair.

Still naked, I opened the door. The water splashed over his shoulders and chest as he turned and held out his arms.

I walked into the warmth of the water and his embrace.

Chapter Sixteen

Orion

I still got a thrill when I saw the flash of an incoming email.

Our offices were just down the hall from each other on the first floor and Holland shot off messages to me as if he couldn't wait with his every thought, or compile them into a coherent end-of-day report.

Holland: *You can't fix the world's problems with more designer blue jeans.*

Me: *Every man should have at least two pair.*

Holland: *I don't.*

Me: *I'll order you a dozen pair. You have a huge closet. I intend to fill it up.*

Holland: *Think you're going to win me over with clothes like you do the others on the farm? Try harder.*

Me: *Already have.*

My incoming banner remained blank. Dark.

The door to my office slowly opened. Holland stood in his old Zilly's uniform, dark trousers, white button-up shirt. The new clothes we'd ordered still hadn't yet arrived.

He stood beside the half open door, eyes storm-dark as always, mouth a smirk. "I'm not wearing clothes half the time these days anyway."

"All right, then. I'll cancel the order."

He came toward me, angling so he half sat, half leaned on the edge of my desk. "Typical Alpha."

"Typical?"

"You just want me naked all the time, isn't that it?"

"Huh. Thought it was the other way around." In truth, Holland had initiated every encounter after our first, mornings, evenings, and afternoons. We got very little work done, but that was what assistants and delegating was for.

We stared at each other, unmoving. The tingles began in my stomach and shot outward to my chest and groin like little lightning flashes. Hunger flared, but not for food. All over, my skin went hot and cold until I could barely stand it anymore.

Holland leaned in and reached for my shirt, immediately starting to unbutton it.

I tilted my head up and our mouths found each other so quick and heated I forgot to breathe.

Over the last few days, this kept happening. And I never wanted it to stop.

Holland sat in my lap and heated me up. Our hands went everywhere. I waited for his usual command.

"Lift me up. Take me upstairs."

He wrapped his arms about my neck and shoulders as I lifted him easily and cradled him to my chest, still madly kissing him.

Where I wanted to go wasn't far. I was young and strong. I flew up the staircase and took him to my own rooms where we spent most of our time together now.

I nearly tripped. He wouldn't let my head up so I couldn't see where I was going.

But we made it to my bed intact. I placed him gently upon the covers and hovered over him, my hands at his shirt and the waist of his trousers.

Holland didn't hesitate to do the same for me, undressing me quickly, and took his time caressing me as I knelt before him, looking down at him. He and I had no worry, or qualm, that it always ended up with him on top.

160

When we were both naked, Holland reached up to touch my cheek, as he often did now, perhaps as if to test that I was solid and real. His hand was so warm and soft, cupping me with a reverence that shone in his flashing eyes.

His other hand delved lower to hard flesh and gripped, moving up and down my shaft. A loud groan escaped my throat.

I sat back, letting his hand have more access, but it was too much. I needed to last. I wanted him ready. I wanted him in me. I couldn't get enough.

I scooted quickly down and gripped his own hardness, pulling it up straight from his body before tonguing the head. Then I drew him into my mouth and felt his entire body tense, then go limp as I sucked him.

When I felt him harden even more, and tasted the sweetness that started to pour out of him, I lifted up and off him. "My turn. Make me ready. I want you in me."

One dark eyebrow quirked against errant, shining bangs. His gaze raked me up and down. "You look ready now."

I turned onto my side and he rolled on top of me, pushing me until I was all the way on my back.

I spread my legs, perhaps a little too eager. But who could be too eager with him? He was amazing, and it was all too obvious I'd fallen for him. He knew it. I knew it. Though no exchange of those magic words had yet happened.

I had always hoped to find an Omega like him. The private houses ministered to my desires when I was in the Burn, but even so, many in the world thought what I wanted and craved from an Omega was an aberration. To be filled by my lover, to be taken. It wasn't proper. It wasn't Alpha-like.

I opened to him readily, because I wanted it, because for me it felt natural. I had taken Holland into me that first time as if it were meant to be. My body naturally drew him in, needing him, craving more. I actually knotted while being penetrated by him that first time.

Had Holland noticed? He had not said a word about that aspect of my sexual response. I worried it could unnerve him, so I'd held back since. But I couldn't control the desire to knot forever.

Holland knelt between my thighs and touched me everywhere. I swelled, pulsed and throbbed for him in a way I'd never experienced with any other Omega.

He kissed me first on the mouth, then on the chest—tonguing my nipples—and moved further down. His slick fingers found my entrance and did their magical dance. My cock bobbed up as he licked all the way down the underside, then up again, taking the head into his mouth.

I trembled all over.

"Please." I didn't care if I was begging. I didn't care about anything except him. Everything about him was luscious, alluring and special.

He knew from past bedroom escapades that if he sucked me too long and too hard I'd come fast and what I really wanted was to come with him inside me.

He laughed as I begged, coming up to kiss me again and placing himself against my opening. I thrust up as he pushed and everything was perfect, gliding, hot and sweet.

I curved my arms around him and held him as his slim hips moved. It was exquisite torture of a fine and pure pleasure I'd known with no one but him.

I felt like I held a sleek and feral mink-boy in my arms, a boy whose wiry strength and small build fit inside me to perfection, and whose coolness and sly critiques of the world thrilled me beyond romance and into my soul.

He drenched me in ecstasy.

Moving faster as he sensed my impending orgasm, Holland took me in hand and stroked.

I lifted my head and shoulders off the bed as I came. He pumped for a few more seconds, and I felt the surge of heat deep inside as he filled me up.

His hand continued to stroke and that was when I felt it.

The knot began to form at the base of my cock.

I could not keep my body from writhing.

Holland pulled out of me with a slow, sweet tug and lifted himself so he could look down. "This happened once before," he said. "Does it mean you need--"

"No. No, I don't have to penetrate you at all." My breaths came fast as the euphoria spiraled through my body. "Just—if you—" I wasn't shy with the cloister Omegas I rented, but with Holland, even after all we'd shared, after I proved to him I really did want him on top, I couldn't say the words.

"It's okay," he said. Smart, as always, he figured things out on his own and had been since I'd met him. Reverent now, he took me in hand and stroked up from the knot.

It felt grand.

He put his other hand around the base of my cock. "Will this hurt you?" he asked, giving a squeeze.

"No, that's good." I tossed my head. The pillow grew damp with my sweat. I closed my eyes and went with the ecstasy, letting the white glitter of it surround me.

Then I felt warmth at the tip. A tongue. A suck, and I was gone.

My cock pulsed and I was coming, the small but firm hands and sweet mouth coaxing the knot up, making me give everything I had.

The orgasm lasted minutes and pleasure tears leaked from my eyes before my knot churned beneath the tip of my cock forcing out more spurts, and deflated.

I couldn't see. I couldn't think.

I felt arms encircle my head, and that sweet mouth upon my neck and chin and cheeks and forehead.

"It's okay now," Holland said.

I reached up, pulling him to me and turning a bit onto my side. "Sometimes I can't stop it." My voice came out thready, exhausted.

"It's okay, I said. Beautiful, actually. You should never stop it if you don't want to. Not on my account."

"I couldn't stop it our first time."

"But you have been holding back since then?"

I nodded once.

"You shouldn't ever do that. Don't do that on my account."

"I didn't want to take advantage."

"I think it's me taking advantage of you. Me who is being rescued. Right?"

"I want more than anything to keep you safe. And for you to know in your heart that I will never hurt you."

"I know that by now," he said smugly. "Wow, your knot was so amazing. I have never envied an Alpha until now."

That didn't sound right to my mind. Envy? "But you are beautiful. Perfect just the way you are. Don't you see that?"

"No. I don't." He bowed his head, nuzzling under my chin.

"You must see it. I'll make you see it. You're perfect."

"I'm very very flawed," he argued.

"Not to me."

"I know. That's why I trust you. You don't see the broken man. You see the real me. I never thought it would be possible I'd meet an Alpha so blind in that way."

"I'm not blind. I have far better than average vision."

"Perhaps." His arms tightened about my shoulders and now his cheek pressed my chest.

I held him as close as possible as we napped.

Chapter Seventeen

Holland

I lay with my head resting on Orion's chest, listening to the life-force of his body thrum. The room, edged in amber light as the afternoon waned, made me feel safe and guarded well, bathed in a golden security I had won when I let myself feel again.

My stomach growled but I didn't want food. I just wanted more Orion.

Orion had a way of making me think differently about myself. Back on the farm, Sen would have probably said he was the best medicine I could have ever received. Everything I thought I was after the attack—tough, hard, hateful, nonchalant, stubborn, cold—melted away in the onslaught of Orion's love.

I still remembered the attack in great detail—how that mad Alpha's hands hurt, how he held me down so hard I couldn't breathe, how he pummeled and tossed me around until I was dazed, until I was too passed out to be not compliant—but thankfully the immediacy of that memory, and the pain and fear associated with it were beginning to fade.

It was hard to describe how the memory still made me feel. Sometimes my heart was a hollow cave. Before coming to Orion's gigantic home, I had always felt as if I were one step away from cardiac arrest. Like I was balanced on a tightrope across an ancient and vast abyss, and I couldn't go forward and I couldn't go back.

But now I saw my way forward better and better with each day.

We hadn't formed a mate-bond to supersede Bosk's yet, but I truly began to believe it could be done. I hadn't told

Orion yet, but I felt that we were right for each other. Perfect together. We'd find a way.

So far, I hadn't felt anything from the supposed weak bond, no unusual force or tingle, nothing from that monstrous source. I hoped it would remain that way until Orion's next Burn. But that wasn't for another month.

I worried about that, but told myself over and over again it would turn out fine. It was Orion, after all. He might be only twenty-three, but he behaved far more mature and aware of himself than his age, and his concern for my well-being so far trumped his own.

I had no worries about his Burn and forming a mate-bond with him.

He slept at my side, one arm flung over my naked waist, his beautiful face relaxed and content.

But of course the idyllic silence couldn't last.

A buzzing sounded from the room's floor. I leaned over the side of the bed. The noise was coming from Orion's pants.

He lifted his head, one arm propping him, and said, "What?"

"Your phone." I gestured toward the floor. "That's awful. You don't have a pretty song programmed on there like everyone else?"

"I don't know. No one ever calls me. And you... you only message me. Or email."

"Old habits," I said.

He slid partway off the bed, exposing his beautiful ass as he fumbled to pick up the phone.

He brought it back up into the bed and my lovely view was destroyed as he pulled the cover to his waist and sat up against the headboard, staring down at the screen.

"Anything important?" I asked.

"It's my lawyer."

"Saben?"

He nodded, poking at the screen.

"You're ignoring me. What's he say?"

"He left a message."

After accessing it, Orion set the phone on his lap and hit speaker.

The old man's voice rang out in the quiet room of our so recent lovemaking.

Orion, this is Saben. You need to call me. Right away. The deal with your claim may be going sour as we speak. This can't wait. I hope you get this immediately, but in case you don't, I'm calling Alston as well.

Where are you anyway?

Call me back now.

My skin turned clammy and cool. I think my heart actually stopped.

Orion met my eyes, his own dark and glassy.

"The claim?" My voice came out hushed. "What does that mean?"

"Shh," Orion said. He put one arm around me and with the other pushed a little phone icon on his screen. "I'm calling him back right now."

Orion kept the phone on the speaker setting, and I heard the ringing. Then the immediate pick up.

"Saben here. Orion, is that you?"

"Yes. I got your message. What's going on?"

"Your very polite and wonderful acquaintance, the Alpha Bosk, has retained a lawyer himself. He challenges your claim based on a prior mate-bond that was never legally acknowledged but nonetheless appears on his own blood test. Did you know about this? He wants you to deliver Holland to him immediately or he will take action."

My head began to ring. Everything got a hazy and faraway look.

"Can you delay that action?"

"I can try. But if the delay is more than a day, I'm sure he will file proprietary charges with the police. They can then come in and take Holland and there's not a thing I can do to help except continue the fight for your claim to be recognized on paper. But if he strengthens the mate-bond and gets it confirmed, then there will be nothing more we can do."

"Do all you can to delay," Orion said.

I barely heard him. My ears buzzed.

"I have managed to get hold of his blood test to look it over. Has Holland ever been tested?"

"Yes."

"The results are not astounding by any sense of that word," Saben continued. "In Bosk's blood the percentage of mate-bond agents is minimal at best. It was a botched attempt at chaining an Omega to him. But it still counts in court. Unless you can show you are his true mate with a one hundred percent result in your own blood test, you could lose."

Silence filled the phone line, and the room.

Finally, as if he were whispering, Orion replied. "My Burn is not due for another month."

"I'm afraid you don't have that kind of time."

More silence.

Saben finally said, "Are you still there?"

"Yes."

"Bosk wants a meeting here at my office. He wants you to come and turn over the Omega then. It's late in the day. I can delay until very late afternoon tomorrow. That's all I can do."

"I understand. I'll contact you tomorrow."

I watched with blurry vision as Orion reached out to the phone's screen and ended the call.

He glanced up and held my gaze. "I don't intend to make that meeting."

My mind swam, but a moment's clarity stung me. "What? You know you can't keep me from him. And if he goes into the Burn himself--"

"He probably hasn't gone into the Burn because of the medication he's taking."

"But if he stops taking it, which he might already have done," I began.

"We can run. I have the resources."

"And become fugitives? Forever? There has to be another way. There has to be a way I can fight for my own right to choose!"

Orion slowly shook his head.

I swallowed hard. I leaned forward and grasped Orion's forearms.

He lowered his face and would not look at me.

"Is there way," I asked. "A way you could induce a Burn?"

Now he glanced up. "I never thought of that."

"Well, hormones cause it. So we trick your body somehow. Make it think you're in the Burn."

"Hormones. Yes! I should have thought of that." He picked up his phone and started scrolling. Then he pressed down hard.

"You're calling Doctor Wilde?"

"I know you don't like him, but he'll help me if he can. He's known me since I was born and he and my dad were good friends. He's always been good to me."

The phone picked up and I heard the voice of Wilde's husband.

"Doctor Wilde's office. Maybe I help you?"

"This is Orion. I need to speak with the doctor right away."

"Can I put you on hold?"

"Yes."

A faintly tinny sound emanated from the phone. Something that perhaps once tried to call itself music.

As we waited, I felt myself lose upper balance just sitting on the side of the bed. My body fell forward until my forehead rested against Orion's chest.

Orion's arms came around me, the fingers of one hand combing through my hair. "No matter what," he whispered into my hair, "he will never have you."

I couldn't imagine hiding with Orion for the rest of my life. If Bosk stood before me right now, and I were holding a gun, I knew I would not hesitate to kill him.

I did not like that aspect of myself, but it was the truth.

Finally, a voice piped up from the phone lying on the spread between us.

"Orion. Good to hear from you. What do you need?"

"My Omega might be taken from me at any moment if I don't create a mate-bond. But my Burn is not due for a month. Is there a way to speed up that process?"

"There is. And I can help you with that. But the hormone shots I would administer to you are different for everyone. And there are side effects."

"Tell me."

As the doctor spoke, I continued to lean against Orion. He held me to him, his hand brushing up and down my spine. But nothing could alleviate the tension. My body was taut, strung tight, my muscles quivering.

Wilde's voice spouted off a hell of a list of problems. Orion could experience stomach aches, headaches, vomiting, no appetite, severe mood swings, weird cravings. But all that seemed normal. Alphas in the Burn were no picnic, even the sane ones from what I'd been told. But when Wilde listed the prolonged side effects which might lead to more severe problems like blood clots or stroke, I balked.

I shut my eyes. I couldn't have him risk his life for me. That would just be stupid. If he died, Bosk would have me anyway.

"I can handle all that," Orion said.

But could I? I took a deep breath and held it.

"How soon can I get the treatment?" Orion asked.

"From your tone I am thinking this is an emergency situation."

"He could be taken from me as soon as tomorrow afternoon."

"Ah, well, I can have you in today if you hurry. My office closes at six."

170

"I'll be there!" Orion pulled back from me, pushing himself from the bed to stand naked beside it.

"But," Wilde added. "I can't guarantee the shot will work that fast. It will induce a Burn, but it could take up to two or three days before you start to feel it."

My hopes fell. A possibility of a stroke and he still might not feel the Burn until it was too late for us!

"Give me the highest dose. I'll be there in half an hour!"

"I won't close up until you get here."

Orion started pulling on his pants.

I sat staring at him as the phone went dark. He was so beautiful. And I was so afraid. The odds still weren't in our favor. I could lose him by this time tomorrow.

Finally, I slid off the bed, still naked, and faced him. "I'll go with you."

"No. You stay here. I'll be back before you know it."

A weird paranoia clutched me. Was he trying to distance himself already? Seeing that it would all go wrong?

There was no way I was letting him out of my sight.

"I want to go!" I grabbed my trousers off the floor and stepped into them.

"No. I want you to stay here. I know you're safe here. Alston will see to it. And the others. I trust them."

My eyes stung. I hadn't cried. Not ever since the attack. I wasn't about to start. "I'm safe with you!"

"I don't know that. I need to get the shot and talk more with Wilde. And see how I feel. I don't want you compromised in any way."

"You don't want me in the way is what you mean," I mumbled.

"I don't want you hurt."

"You told me twice now, and I believe you. You will never hurt me. Please."

He came to me, putting his hands on my shoulders and looking down at me with such a pained gaze. "Do this one thing my way. Wait for me here. You are never and will never be in my way. I simply want you protected, and if you're here, I know you will be. It's one less worry."

Stupidly, it made sense.

I backed up a step, dropping my shirt to the floor. I nodded. "I'm a worry. I know."

"No." He came toward me again, clasping me tighter. "You're not!" He put his arms all the way around me and hugged me to him.

"Fine," I grumbled into his chest.

I hated this. But I wasn't about to go anywhere I wasn't wanted.

When he finally backed away to finish dressing, I held my chin high. I made myself stand firm and never show my anxiety and horror at this whole mess.

I quickly fastened my pants, realizing I actually needed a shower before dressing. And Orion, he had no time for that. We both probably stunk of wild sex. I almost wanted to laugh.

Orion finished dressing and turned for the door.

"Orion."

He swung back to face me.

"It's going to work. We'll make it work." I stood defiant, though I couldn't keep the note of desperation from my voice.

His face was emotionless. His stance rigid. Then he strode toward me so fast and I caught my breath as he clasped my face between his hands.

"You do understand what all this means," he said, his brow lowering.

I nodded, turning my face into his left open palm and kissing it.

He shook me very gently. "I mean it. You do know. The mate-bond between Alpha and Omega cannot be formed in the way--" He gulped. "In the way we've been together."

I pressed my lips tight and breathed in hard through my nose.

His right hand moved down my face to caress my jaw and neck. "I told you I would never harm you and that you were safe with me. But you aren't."

"I am," I protested.

"You are safer with me than with *him*. But that still doesn't make you safe."

"By birth, I never was," I replied.

He winced.

I reached out and clasped my arms around his waist. I looked up at him, my lips an inch from his chin. "We will make this work. You and I. Together. We will."

He lowered his chin and our lips met.

Then he left me standing in the middle of his room, turned and walked out the door.

I wondered what would be coming back to me. My Alpha lover? Or an Alpha turned mad from the Burn?

Chapter Eighteen

Orion

I sat gripping the armrest of the limo's leather couch, staring at the fridge and thinking about the alcohol that resided within. But with whatever cocktail of hormones that was running through my veins, I didn't dare.

The ride to Wilde's office went quickly because I told the driver to go fast. But the ride home seemed endless.

I could not get Holland's wide-eyed gaze from my mind. He'd stood tall, chin up, demanding as usual. But those eyes had held too much of a storm kept at bay.

This would not be easy between us. We shared intimacy, caring and on my part, love. He had given to me his trust and his true virginity. The past few days we'd been unable to keep our hands off each other.

But this would test us. Me in the Burn and him needing to bend when I knew it was the very last thing he wanted. But there was no other way for the bond to form.

For myself, I didn't need Omegas to bend for me to assuage the Burn. I preferred to have them on top. I was aberrant that way. Now when I needed to do everything right by Holland, what if I lacked the skills?

I stared out the limo windows at the dusk, the lights of the streets and other cars flashing by. It seemed to take forever, this journey, and I needed to be back home now.

I searched my body for any sign that the hormones Wilde had given me were affecting me. It was too early, of course, but I still catalogued every quirk of my body: heart beating a little faster, mouth a bit dry, muscles tense, a twinge in my groin. Did I smell any different? It would take another person to let me know that.

By the time we pulled up the drive to home, I was exhausted from my own nervous thinking.

Inside, I expected Holland to be waiting for me at the door. But there was no one. I immediately checked the dining room. Nothing.

Alston came to me in the hallway and said, "If you are looking for him, he's at the pool."

I raised my eyebrows in question, but he shrugged as if to say he had no clue why.

It was still too cold to swim. But then I remembered a pool was Holland's favorite place for comfort. It was the place we'd first met and spoke while he sat in the slatted shadows of the patio, a shadow himself mixing with the dust motes and rusty, pre-autumn light.

I moved quickly through the house and came to the patio door. It was ajar.

Holland sat with his knees drawn to his chest, staring out over the still water of the long, azure pool. The lights were on in the water, making it glow in the early evening darkness. A faint chlorine scent shifted on the breeze along with cut grass and the faded fragrance of the old rose bush that grew beyond the patio gate.

As he heard my footsteps, Holland sat straight up and held out his hand. "Orion! You're back. How do you feel?"

I took his hand and sat on the edge of the lounge chair beside him. Our sides pressed warmly. I wanted to take him into my arms and hold him forever.

"I'm fine."

I heard him gulp.

"I was thinking," Holland said. "If you don't feel the Burn by tomorrow afternoon, we'll lie and say we're bonded. They'll take our blood but it will be another day before they can get the results. It will buy us time."

I stroked the back of his neck. "That's good thinking."

My voice remained calm, but inside my thoughts whirled, and everything felt out of control.

He leaned his head against my shoulder. "Would having more sex help stir things up?"

I couldn't say no to him. "Maybe."

I kissed him on the side of the head, my lips brushing his soft, silken hair. But my body was so taut and stressed I could barely think. Just the thought of losing him—my instinct was to fight, not fuck, a word I rarely used but at this point in time it seemed appropriate.

I had terrible, dark thoughts. I wanted to break Bosk in two, then bury him out back in the dark with only the owls as witnesses.

"Let's go in," Holland whispered.

We ended up in the dining room while the servants brought in platters of chicken, bowls of soup, and trays of fresh fruit. It all lacked flavor to my palette.

I brought out the whiskey afterward, and Holland said not one word, matching his drinking with my own, glass after glass of magical brown liquid.

I felt nothing. Tipsy maybe. Uneasy. But I never got fully drunk.

In my bed that night, he touched me everywhere but I could not respond. "I'm sorry. I'm sorry," I kept saying.

He put his hand over my mouth. "Don't apologize. Everything you've done for me--" His words faded away.

Later, he kissed my lips softly and said, "Hold me."

Our naked bodies slid together. I clutched him tight to my chest. I breathed his essence and rubbed my face in his beautiful hair.

I didn't see sleep until the curtains began to lighten with the coming dawn.

*

All morning I tried not to chastise myself. I felt no ability to function sexually. No hint of the Burn.

Had Wilde given me a placebo?

Holland would not leave my side. He followed me everywhere, his mood curt but polite, quiet. He seemed almost his normal self, but I knew he was as tangled up inside as I was. Probably more so. He was the one who would suffer at the hand of a madman.

I still wanted to run, hide, leave this place forever. He refused.

By noon we were down to hours before we had to meet with Saben.

I turned to Holland. "I'll go to the meeting by myself. I'll hide you. Tell them all you're my bond-mate and that my ultimatum as such is that Bosk will never see you again."

"That might work. Until he demands a public blood test and finds out the truth."

"The truth is, he doesn't have a true bond with you!"

Holland gazed at me. "I know."

"Why can't they all see that? Why would anyone force you to go off with a maniac?"

Suddenly, the look on Holland's face hardened. "Welcome to my world."

"Damn it, I've been in your world since I met you. That's why I can't let this happen!"

I reached out and put my arms around him. He went stiff, but allowed it.

"Please," I begged. "Let me hide you! Let's both hide."

"Forever?"

"Yes!"

How could I ever *ever* give him up?

He leaned back in my arms to again look at me, his dark blue gaze unwavering. "Too many people depend on you. The servants you employ. The experts you hire. And all the Omegas at Zilly's. For them, we can't hide. You can't hide. You have to be here to make things better. For everyone."

His words made sense, of course, but not to me. Not to my heart.

"I cannot, will not see you turned over to him!"

I pulled back, blind with my emotion, and found myself rushing down the long hall.

"Orion! Where are you going?"

I couldn't think anymore. I just need to move. To go somewhere. And then I knew.

"Alston," I called.

He was at my side in seconds. "Sir?"

"Call the driver. I'm going out!"

"Yes, sir."

"Orion!" Holland came up to me. "Where are you going?"

I would not allow myself to look at him. I turned away and flung the front door open.

The world met my gaze, a normal day with the skies clear blue and a soft breeze waving through the oleanders and the tops of the trees. All the colors of my yard: green grass, silver-green trees, blue horizon, pink flagstone drive seemed brighter, brilliant and yet none of it mattered. It could all collapse to ash right now for all I cared.

As I strode down the path, I heard Holland following.

"Orion!" He raised his voice just enough to make my heart jolt.

I kept walking, and turned to see the limo pulling up the side drive from the garage.

As I got to the edge of the flagstones, a strong hand gripped my arm from behind.

"Ori! Stop!"

He'd never called me that before. And in such a livid, angry tone.

I didn't want to look at him. To see his fury. It would stop me from what I was determined to do.

"What are you doing?"

I yanked away from his grip.

When I didn't answer his question, he said, "If you're going to confront him, then I'm going, too!"

No! I wouldn't do that to him. But he'd guessed correctly. I knew Bosk's address. If I could get to him before the meeting--

"What are you going to do? Kill him? And then be brought up on murder charges?" Holland grabbed my arm again, swiftly spinning me to face him. "No! Besides, if anyone kills him, it should be me. But we're not going to do that."

"Why not?" I couldn't see him clearly. My vision was breaking up. Not tears. I was too angry for tears. But rage. The blackness of it starting to hone in on the sides, and my focus continually trying to adjust.

"Orion. Listen to me. I had time to think all night and today. Even if I go with him, even if the worst were to happen to me and he forced himself on me again." He paused. Swallowed. His eyes became shiny. "Even if that happened, I'd fight that bond. I did before. It didn't take. I feel nothing and the agents in the blood are minimal. I'll fight it again. Bonds are more than physical anyway. Everyone says it. They're emotional. I feel only rage toward that man. Only hate. We would never fully bond. Never. And you can fight it in court and say that. And then you'll get me back."

"I won't let it go down that way." Gruff, hoarse, my throat threatened to close.

Holland took both my hands in his, holding them tight.

"You don't get to choose. I do. Much as I want it, there won't be any killing. Not today. Hopefully not any day."

I tried to pull back from him again, but he wouldn't allow it.

"If you do this," Holland said. "I swear. I'll never speak to you again."

I blinked hard, realizing my breaths came fast as if I'd been running.

"No! I have to confront him. I want the Challenge."

"My love." His voice had softened. "The Challenge has been outlawed for over three hundred years."

"I want it!"

"I know." He tugged at my hands. "Come back inside. Please."

I was shaking now. But I had to follow him. He commanded my every move and thought just by being alive. He was more the Alpha in this relationship than I had ever been.

I left the limo quietly humming, and blindly followed him back inside.

Everything was too bright, too painful, too much. The hormones had made my sensitivity increase, but I still didn't feel the Burn. My skin didn't heat. My cock remained limp inside my trousers.

Holland led me upstairs to my room. He sat me down on my bed, then crawled over me until I fell back. He pressed himself to me and held me.

He held me until my shaking subsided.

Chapter Nineteen

Holland

We lay in the afternoon shadows of Orion's room listening to each other breathe, our hands clasped side by side. Waiting. Waiting for the moment we had to get up and go to Saben's offices to see if we had any legal ground left to stand on.

Though Orion showed his rage, there was still no sign of the Burn within him.

I felt a strange, odd calm surround me. The prospect of seeing Bosk should have terrified me. Instead, I felt mostly disgust, and a sense inside myself that I would do whatever it took to win Orion back. I did not accept my fate with Bosk, but I had accepted that I could endure it.

Neither of us said a word. I glanced at the clock to the side of the bed. We had another half hour before we had to leave. My heart went into my throat before I calmed myself again, before my breathing leveled out.

Orion's hand squeezed mine, feeling my stress.

As I closed my eyes, his phone went off.

He sat up partway to remove it from his pocket and look at it.

"It's Saben," he said to me.

I sat up as he answered and put the phone on speaker.

"Orion!"

"Here."

"A little change of plan. Have you left yet?"

"Not yet."

"Good. We're all meeting at the courthouse. I got an appointment at the last minute with a judge. He will hear us out. My argument. Your argument."

Orion inhaled sharply. "What time?"

"Four. You'll have to leave now."

I was already up and running to the bathroom to wash my face and comb my hair.

When Orion walked in he stared at my reflection in the mirror.

"This is better news, right?" I asked.

"Maybe. At least we will be heard by an impartial party."

"Good."

Before, all we could hope was that we might convince Bosk, through our lawyers at the meeting, to make him give up his claim. Now, we had a judge. An Alpha judge, but still a judge.

The limo had stayed parked in the drive at the end of the front path. It was ready for us as soon as we walked out the door.

Orion held my hand tightly. I squeezed back as hard as I could.

He looked at me as the driver opened the doors for us. "I cannot lose you."

"No matter what, you never will," I said.

*

Everything was new to me. Alien and strange. I'd been off the farm for only a matter of days. Eight to be exact. In that time, I'd experienced so much: outrage and fear, gratitude and wonder, and falling in love. My emotions had tested me. But I had very little experience, still, of the real world.

I'd never seen a courthouse except in videos.

We drove up and passed a little gate that forced the driver to take a ticket before it would open to let us in. We entered a dark tunnel. On either side I could see parked cars everywhere in lines. Up ahead was a curb and a sidewalk. The many lights here were white, everything lit up.

The limo pulled up to the curb and the driver got out to open our door.

182

Glass doors led inside the building to a lobby.

Everything was bright and glassy and shiny. We had to walk through a security scan.

Orion emptied his pockets into a plastic container.

I had nothing on me, so I walked through first and waited for him, nearly trembling, on the other side.

Saben was waiting for us as he turned into a lobby area, and he came right up saying, "This way. This way."

He led us to another set of doors and opened them, ushering us inside.

The room was smaller than I expected, with a low ceiling, no windows, and beige walls. A few rows of seats flanked two sides of a single aisle, a large, tall judge's table up front, a witness booth, and two long tables facing front.

I saw two people sitting at one of the tables. No judge yet. And no one sitting in any of the rows.

I didn't want to look at the two other people because I knew right away one of them would be Bosk. I had worked hard to wall away the memory of him, of his wild manic look, his hard, unseeing eyes, and the way his lips had curled back showing sharp, uneven teeth. I had willed away the impressions of his hard fingers poking into me, his bites, his strength as he shoved me hard against a wall, a floor, ignoring the mattress that was in the mating room for his use.

I didn't care if Bosk was on medication now. I didn't care if he seemed under control. It didn't matter if they called him ill, or if his Burn gave him legal leeway for his unimaginably destructive behavior. His violence had been a choice. I hated him for it.

As Orion and Saben moved forward, and the two Alphas at the other table turned toward us, I froze. I couldn't take another step.

Orion reached back for me, noticing I was no longer close, and turned.

Our eyes met and I shook my head. I'd changed my mind. I couldn't go through with this. I couldn't let Bosk take me back. I'd felt strong all day long, but now everything started to crumble around me, all my inner compartments and walls bursting open, falling away to rubble.

Orion came toward me, his arms open, ready to catch me if I fell.

But I managed not to collapse. My cheeks flamed. My heart pounded.

Orion glanced over his shoulder at Saben, who had turned my way.

"We have to stop this," Orion whispered. "He can't go on. We can't do this to him. It's our responsibility as Alphas to keep Omegas like him safe. What is happening here?"

"Tell that to the judge in exactly those words," Saben said.

I can do this. I can do this. I kept repeating that thought in my mind over and over until I heard nothing else.

"Holland, you must go on. We have a chance to win this. Orion has to take this chance. You have to take it," Saben said to me.

I did not trust other Alphas yet, not even Orion's own personal house staff, but when I looked at Saben's pleading eyes, the muscles soft and relaxed about the edges, I could see he told the truth. He was savvy or Orion would not have kept him on as his lawyer after his dad's death. There was conviction in those dark depths. This lawyer would fight.

I swallowed, my mouth dry, and cleared my throat. Finally, I found the will to reach out and take Ori's hand. *Ori.* I had started thinking of him as Ori only today, only after I realized I'd truly given him my whole heart. All the way.

No one could ever take that away from me. From us.

Ori took my hand in his and together the three of us went to the long table on the left and took our seats.

Soon a bailiff entered from a side door up front.

"All hail, Judge Powers. Rise."

We all stood.

I still refused to look over at the other two Alphas.

A man in a black gown entered the room. He had a rather round, placid face and white hair. He had to have been old. At least a hundred and fifty, probably more. Some Alphas lived as long as two hundred years or more.

The judge walked up some steps to his high seat over his lofty desk and faced us.

An older Omega walked in, then. I was shocked. He went to a chair by the judge and turned on a computer. I now understood he was the judge's recorder, but I had no idea he would be an Omega. But of course Omegas lived lives outside farms and group homes. The mated ones had families and even, sometimes, jobs. I should not have been surprised.

Before I could think further on it, the bailiff announced our case.

Justice Powers looked at a small screen to one side, then looked out at us, first at the table to our right, then toward us.

His white brows came together in a fluffy line. "Two claims. One Omega," he said. "Well, let's see here. The claim that comes first is usually the winner."

I heard a chair scrape back. Bosk's lawyer stood. "Your Honor, my client's claim supersedes that because of the mate-bond."

"A mate-bond?" Justice Powers asked. "Why, then, is your Omega claimed by another?"

"The story is a long one, to be sure," the lawyer said.

"Well, that's why we're here." Justice Powers leaned back and put his hands behind his head. "Do tell."

It was all going far more casually than I expected. I was both fascinated and horrified that this case was being approached as a run of the mill session, as if a person's life— mine—was not at stake.

The lawyer for Bosk began to tell, in a long and boring monotone, the story of how Bosk had hired me at Zilly's and a mate-bond had formed between us during his Burn. He mentioned nothing about Omegas having to gas the room to stop him from killing me. And nothing about my injuries, or Bosk's untreated, mental aberrations.

Powers glanced at the file, frowning.

Saben took that moment to stand. "Your Honor, if I may."

Powers held out his hand to quiet him. "You'll get your side told in a moment."

He glanced toward Bosk and his lawyer. "I have the blood test right here in the file. You do understand the mate-bonds are rated."

"Uh, yes, your Honor."

"There's a one to ten scale. The ideal, of course, is a ten. If a bond is still forming, or formed under the wrong conditions, or duress, it might be a one or a two. In between are those who are willing but not quite there yet, a still-forming evolution of a relationship our country holds in highest esteem, and a bond that will hopefully last a lifetime."

Silence.

"This blood test shows a 1.2 mate-bond status."

"Your Honor," interrupted the lawyer. "The law still says--"

"Do not lecture me on the law."

All of a sudden my entire body relaxed from rock hard tension to a release that made it feel like I was taking in air for the first time in hours. I looked at that Alpha judge putting the real facts before him, and realized maybe I had a chance. Maybe.

"Your Honor," said the lawyer. "The bond to the Omega Holland was formed prior to the claim made by Orion Callahan."

"But," said Powers, "the claim to that bond, which I remind you is a 1.2 rating, was made after the first claim of Orion Callahan."

I heard him mutter under his breath before saying, "Yes."

"And the Burn has not yet called this Omega to your client's side."

"No, sir. He is on medication that temporarily prevents the Burn."

"That must be some strong medication. Burns are not easily circumvented."

"It's all in the report, your Honor."

Powers seemed to ignore the statement. He shuffled a few papers, then turned his attention onto us.

"I see your client's claim on this Omega is pre-dated to the claim of Bosk Altimarian."

Saben stood. "It is, your Honor."

"And the Omega is here today in this court?" The judge glanced directly at me.

"He is, your Honor."

"I am aware of this Omega's records. Including medical. The big question here is if the bond was made under duress."

"If you allow it, he will testify it was, your Honor," Saben answered.

"I wasn't finished. If he would not mind taking the stand, I have some questions I'd like to ask him."

"I have some questions as well," Bosk's lawyer said abruptly.

Powers turned toward him. "Did I indicate you could speak?"

Inwardly, I smiled. Still wary, I was willing to take the stand. A month ago, even a week ago, I probably would have been in no shape to speak in a court like this. But now, with Orion at stake, and my heart, I'd do anything.

"If you will." Powers nodded at me, and the bailiff came to escort me to the witness chair.

Eyes straight ahead. Head clear. Body balanced and under my control. I swore to myself I would not look at Bosk.

Ori looked worried, watching me go, body poised as if to grab, embrace, and whisk me away. I gave him a little nod, and he leaned back, perhaps a bit more relaxed.

I took the stand and looked up at Judge Powers.

He made me state my name and swear to tell the truth. Then he took no time in delving into his questions.

"I have your medical file here, and the date. It was on that date you received these injuries?" He began to read them off. Broken wrist, fractured ribs, various sprains, bruises and contusions. He also mentioned the tearing of the anus in three places.

I felt my face warm, but I continued to stare straight up at his face.

"Those injuries were received on that date?"

"Yes."

"Where?"

"In the mating hall of Zilly's Omega farm."

"Did you consent to the mating of Alpha Bosk?"

I hesitated. Of course, I had. I had gone to my first time willingly, as all Omegas were trained to do. I expected to service an Alpha in his Burn.

"Yes," I replied, clearing my throat.

"So you went willingly to do your duty as an adult Omega on the farm."

"Yes."

"What happened after that?"

I cleared my throat again. My skin began to feel clammy. My back and thighs began to sweat. "I entered the room. As soon as the door closed and the privacy light came on, he—he grabbed me and shoved me against the wall. He immediately tore my clothes. He called me a whore and pushed me to the floor. I—I tried to get up. I was going to ask him if he would wait a minute. I needed to ready myself. I needed to go a little slower. But he started punching me, and I fell flat on my face. I—he—" I stopped.

"Take your time," said the judge.

"He knocked me hard in the head and the room started to spin, and I felt him—I felt him pull me up by the hair. He grabbed my hand and twisted it. I heard—I heard the bone break." My wrist throbbed as the memory came back fully.

"I couldn't move. I couldn't hear him to obey his commands. He shoved me hard against the wall and my ankle gave way. I started to fall. He—put his fingers in me, jammed

188

them hard, then something else. Himself. I felt myself tear. I was screaming, I think, I couldn't hear anymore. He—he punched my head and face over and over as he—as he raped me."

"That's quite enough," Powers said.

I watched his face for any reaction. I couldn't believe I'd said it. All of it. Confessed out in the open in a court, in a room consisting of five Alphas and an Omega. And me.

I felt like I was floating somewhere above my head. Not really there, but apart from it all. I pressed my hands to the tops of my thighs to feel something. Anything. I realized I was jiggling my feet up and down. I pressed my palms hard into the thigh muscles to stop the motion.

Out the corner of my eye I saw Bosk's lawyer jump up. "Your Honor, I have questions."

Powers said, "Sit down."

"But, your Honor, I--"

"I said to sit!"

To me, the judge said, "You may go back to your seat."

The bailiff came up and escorted me back to the table where Ori and Saben sat.

Judge Powers scratched his head and read his little screen for about thirty seconds. The courtroom was silent. Too silent. My stomach began to ache.

I didn't dare move to look at Ori, or anyone. I stared straight ahead, still feeling not quite present inside my body.

The truth was I had consented. I knew it. Add to that, Omegas have no rights, and I still wasn't sure what the outcome might be. A judge had laws to abide by. Justice was supposed to be blind.

I couldn't think anymore. I couldn't see. I could barely breathe.

Finally, the judge gave a little cough and began to speak.

"Omega Holland. Do you want to go with Alpha Bosk Altimarian?"

"No, I do not." My voice sounded like an echo coming from far away.

"I don't know why cases like this one come across my desk. I don't understand it." He turned to Bosk and his lawyer. "Honestly, why would you ever want someone who did not want you back?"

The lawyer started to stand to respond. But Powers shook his head. "Stay seated please. I am talking."

He rubbed at his forehead. He leaned forward and scanned us all. "The mate-bond is one of the most sacrosanct pacts of our country… and in the world. There is nothing that can come between an Alpha and his Omega in their time of need for one another, and during an Alpha's Burn their call to one another is said to be stronger than even the call of death. You've heard the stories of Omegas breaking down walls to get to their Alphas in need, or traveling long distances until their feed bleed and their lungs seize to answer the call. And the same can be said for Alphas. They will go to any length to be with their Omega during their time."

As Powers took a breath, I saw in my peripheral vision Bosk's lawyer begin to nod.

"Even another claim legally made before the bonded Alpha and Omega can file their own claim cannot bar the way for them to be together, especially during the great need of the Burn."

My hopes began to disintegrate as the words fell into me, forming a picture I did not like.

I heard from Bosk's table loud exhales, and a tapping of excited fingers on a wooden tabletop.

Saben bowed his head.

Ori's mouth fell open in shock.

I remained still, chin up, my spirit hovering about two feet to my left.

Powers tilted his head at me.

"That said," he began. "Those words about tearing down walls, etcetera, etcetera are spoken about Alphas and Omegas in full, pure mate-bonds, where the souls meet and intertwine. It sounds mystical and full of silly poetry, but it is not silly at all. Those who have it know of what I speak. There is nothing like it under the sun. I would not sully the bond I have with my own Omega by ever thinking, or decreeing otherwise. This bond is rated a 1.2 out of a possible ten. Add to that the fact it was created under duress. A 1.2, under official law, is still considered a bond, but it is, in the eyes of this court, incomplete. One party of this bond has testified he has no desire to complete the bond. Therefore, we are back to the claims."

He reached up and scratched at his head again, a habit he seemed to have.

"The claim of Alpha Orion Callahan pre-dates the claim of Alpha Bosk Altimarian."

Powers picked up his gavel. "I rule in favor of Alpha Orion Callahan that his claim to the Omega Holland is valid and legal. The claim of Bosk Altimarian is hereby denied."

Just like that, it was over.

The bailiff asked us to rise as the judge exited. I barely heard him.

Had we won? Yes, we had won. I knew it logically. But emotionally, internally, I had not yet processed it. Judge Powers did not uphold the bond, after his whole speech about sacrosanct mate-bonds. It had come down to the claims. Ori's illegal claim. Bought and paid for and never questioned.

I stood on shaky legs. Nearby, I heard a hiss. As I reacted, my head turning, I saw Bosk.

He was even larger and taller than I remembered, easily two hundred seventy five pounds, his eyes cold and small, peering at me from beneath two bushy, thick eyebrows.

His face contorted as he looked straight at me. "This isn't over," he snarled. "You watch your ass from now until forever, filthy whore Omega!"

"You stay away from him!" Ori yelled.

Bosk's lawyer grabbed his arm and practically pulled him out of the room.

Saben said, "I'll file a restraining order first thing in the morning."

I rocked back. Ori caught me in his arms and pulled me tight, my back to his chest.

"I'm yours?" I asked in a whisper.

Saben chuckled and gave me a wink.

"You're mine," Ori said, and lifted me off my feet as he hugged me tighter.

"We did it," Saben said with a laugh. "And I didn't even have to speak. I'm still billing you though."

"Of course," said Ori. He let me down and turned me around so we were face to face.

"How do you feel?" he asked me.

"I still feel like I'm outside myself. Like this is a dream."

"It's no dream, I assure you. I did all the paperwork," Saben said.

Ori ran a hand down the side of my face. "You'll be okay now. I'll make sure. No one will ever hurt you again."

I felt a warm tear splash onto my cheek. I didn't feel like I was crying. Not at all. But when Ori took a handkerchief from his pocket to wipe my face, it came away soaked.

Chapter Twenty

Orion

Holland smiled down at me and it was beautiful. Lips pink over white teeth. Cheeks slightly flushed. He had so rarely smiled in the short time we'd been together.

"I still think I'm dreaming," he said.

"A nightmare."

"A nightmare that turned good," he replied.

We had just made love.

We had been waiting that night for the Burn to come over me from the hormone shots. But we couldn't keep our hands to ourselves.

Now Holland sat at my side and stroked my hair. "Feel anything yet?"

He had asked me that same question three times in the past two hours.

"I know you're worried," I replied with a sigh.

"Not worried."

"If you are, don't be. There are many ways for me to get through the Burn."

"What do you mean? I'm here for you. I'm not worried."

"What I mean is--" I hesitated. Everything seemed to be happening so fast. I hated to broach the subject of me being on top. "I don't have to, you know, be on top to get through it."

Holland frowned. "But to form the mate-bond it must be that way."

"You're safe now. It's not an imperative if you can't."

"I want the mate-bond. I want you to eradicate everything that monster left behind in my blood. You've done so much for me, and I know it's probably too much to ask for more, but I need this." His breath caught and shuddered in his chest.

I reached up to him and pulled him down to me. "I want the mate-bond, too. But I thought it might be too soon for you."

Holland closed his eyes tight for a moment. "You won't hurt me. I know it. Will it be so hard?"

"Not for me," I said.

"I know you don't prefer it. Being on top," he said, opening his eyes.

I stared up at him. "It doesn't matter what I prefer. This is about you. I know you don't wish to be touched—uh—like that."

"With you, it won't be a terrible thing." He gave me a fast smile and took a deep breath. "Will it be for you?"

"No! Not at all. But to mate-bond, it will include a knot. Are you sure it won't harm you?"

He smiled. "I'm an Omega. I'm made for that. I'll be all right with you inside me like that. And because it's you, I will love everything you do and every way you touch me."

"I want to know you are sure. I don't want you to do it against your will. Or because you think you must."

"I wouldn't do that. I want this, Ori. How many ways can I say it?"

"All right. I hear you."

"Then we won't wait. We'll form the mate-bond as soon as the Burn takes you." His face closed in for a moment. "Unless *you* want to wait?"

I raised my arms up to his shoulders, his skin silken against my palms. "I don't want to wait. I thought maybe you would."

He shook his head. "I'd do it right now." He let out a laugh. It sounded a bit nervous.

"You can still be on top when we do it," I whispered.

"Yes. I know."

We both laughed then. He pressed himself against my side, his head on my shoulder, and I held him to me thinking I

194

never wanted to let go. I wondered if it was possible the bond was forming even now, emotionally, psychically.

When it did actually become real, with a rating of ten, would we dream the same dreams? Read each other's thoughts? If we were ever separated, would we claw our way back to each other no matter what?

With Holland, I knew I would want to feel all of that. So quickly, he'd become everything to me, from the defiant boy by the pool I'd first met six months ago to this irresistible and challenging young man in my arms.

When we fell asleep, I swore I could feel him with me in my dreams.

*

Some time in the night, I woke drenched in my own sweat, aroused and trembling.

Holland slept on, and I let him for about half an hour, just holding him as I trembled. Loving the feel of his naked body against mine, relaxed, real, neither one of us demanding anything from the other.

I was happier than I could ever remember feeling. No more cloister Omegas for rent. My true mate was with me. I could feel the truth of it in my mind and heart, in the heated blood that coursed through my veins, in the way my skin prickled everywhere his body touched mine.

Holland shifted in my arms. He made a sweet, questioning sound, muffled by sleep, before lifting his head in the darkness as if trying to see me.

"Ori?"

I pressed myself to him, nuzzling his forehead. "Yes."

"Is it happening now?"

Such a strangely innocent question coming from him. He was always so sure of himself. He'd been the one to first initiate a kiss.

"How did you know?" My voice cracked.

He sat up. "Your body is wet. You didn't shower... oh, you're so hot."

He ran his hand down my slick belly to my groin, feeling that I was harder than I'd ever been, cupping my balls. "Oh," he said, pressing himself against me.

I wasn't sure what to say, really. I didn't feel out of control at all. I never did during my Burns. I was one of those Alphas who had short, sharp fevers with extended arousal that lasted about a day, or two at most. I never lost my mind. I never felt confused or in a daze or a dream—at least no more than what one normally felt in the heat of desire. It was wonderful, of course, but I could still function, eat, walk, talk.

Some Alphas totally lost themselves, but the fogs of euphoria still didn't make them dangers. The worst, labeled *dangerous*, might lose all control and hurt an Omega. When discovered, they were labeled and sometimes they could get help. Strong medications to stave off Burns were usually steeped with side-effects. They were prescribed only in cases of severe mental illness, such as in the case of Bosk. So the only other kind of help available to dangerous Alphas was psychological. From what I'd heard, the success rates weren't great.

My symptoms were among average: hypersexual arousal and a low-grade fever. Like most Alphas, I could get myself to and from a potential partner without incident. I paid, I felt little more than physical pleasure for my partners, and I left when the fever burned itself out. It never occurred to me to ever attempt a mate-bond even on those rare times I did top and produce a knot. No hint of a mate-bond ever happened. The fact that Bosk had intentionally done this to Holland in a frenzy of mania while inflicting pain would continue to infuriate me for the rest of my life.

Holland said softly, sliding his thighs over mine and letting his belly rub against my cock, "Mate-bond me, Ori, so I never have to think of that monster again."

I ran my hands along his smooth waist. "Is that the only reason?"

196

"No." He leaned in to kiss me. "I want it. With you and only you. Always."

"Extreme emotion helps create it."

"I have extreme emotion." His quiet voice soaked through the darkness. "For you."

He didn't yell his love off the rooftops, but his tone held an echoing depth of feeling that brought a sting to my eyes.

"Me, too."

We'd had months of getting to know each other, even if most of it was long-distance. But it was as if we'd always been together. As if it were meant to be.

I pulled the lube we'd been using out from under one of the pillows and cradled it between us.

"This once, unless you decide otherwise, will be like this… me inside you. I promise never to hurt you, and I will never demand it from you now or in the future. It's all your choice. You have the control. Are we clear?"

"Stop talking," he said, his breath against my cheek. "You talk too much."

"You think these things," I responded. "But they need to be stated aloud."

"I know you won't hurt me."

My cock throbbed. I loved Holland inside me, and my secret nature as an Alpha was to bottom, but now the prospect of merging with him, pumping into him as I my fever rose, made the blood in my veins surge hotter than ever.

"I don't know that," I said, lifting him a little so I could see into his eyes through the dim glow of the bathroom nightlight. "When I knot, it won't be easy, even for someone, uh…" I gulped.

"Unscarred?" He finished the sentence for me, tossing his head. "But you must knot me for the mate-bond. Plus, I want it. No, I demand it."

"The contraceptives you received at Zilly's were in your food. You haven't eaten that food in almost two weeks. You could also become pregnant."

Silence for a moment. Then, "I would be honored to carry your child."

It was hard for me to believe him, after all he'd fought to maintain his sanity, and his not-so-secret rage against Alphas.

I sat up, shifting him on my lap. My cock pulsed and I could not hold back a groan.

"You must promise me if it hurts, if you feel there might be damage, to tell me right away. I will stop. I can stop. I'm not a crazed Alpha in the Burn. Do you understand? You must tell me. I won't have you suffer. I won't knot you if you can't take it."

"I will tell you."

By the sound of those words, I knew he wouldn't.

I sighed.

He grabbed the lube from my hand. "You talk so so much," he said. "Just love me, Ori. It will work. I know it will."

He was only five years younger than I, but it seemed like more. He was so young. He thought he knew so much, and after what he'd been through, I'll admit he knew more than most Omegas his age. But neither of us could know for sure that this would work between us. The mating. The bonding.

"May I?" he asked, reaching across the bed toward the lamp. "I want to see you."

"I would like it," I replied. I wanted to see him, too.

He turned on the lamp, which cast the room in golden sheen.

I gripped his waist as he turned until his back was to me. Then he bent before me, letting me see him as I never had, his buttocks parting, his body waiting.

He was slim and young, so his crack was narrow, already revealing the beauty of him, his entrance, his tiny brownish-pink bud surrounded by a thin frame of short, dark hair.

Omegas made their own lubricant within their bodies, but never enough for an Alpha Burn. For that, they needed extra.

I held the lube in my hand and started to open it, but on impulse set it aside for the moment and leaned forward. I put my hands on his upper thighs, my fingers rising to spread him further, bent my head and ran my tongue from his tailbone to his balls.

He drew in a sharp breath.

I then tongued his sweet pink bud, teasing it over and over, poking my tongue inside as far as I could get it.

His body shuddered.

"Ori!"

As I tongued him and lightly sucked, I put one of my hands between his legs and caressed his balls. I moved it further up and felt he was already hard.

I pulled his long cock back and lowered my head from his crack. I could see the reddened tip in the lamplight, wet and leaking, and from behind him I sucked it into my mouth.

He lowered his head just as I heard him wail into a pillow.

My own cock dripped in empathy.

I sucked him until I felt he could take no more and when I let go his cock bobbed back between his legs and up against his belly. I laved his crack again, then pulled back to open the lube. I spread it liberally over his hole and on my fingers and cock.

Slowly, I oiled him up, pressing the tip of my forefinger gently into him. His muscles sucked it in. He made no protest of pain or other difficulty.

I tried to take my time and not hurry, but my cock ached. I wanted to be inside him now. I wanted to mate him. The instinct vibrated through me stronger than I'd ever felt.

Two fingers went into him. "Tell me how that feels."

"Stretching me is not painful so far. If done slow and right, it shouldn't be for any Omega."

I wiggled my fingers and pushed them deeper, stroking everywhere they would reach.

"Oh." The word burst from him. "That's good!"

Omegas experienced pleasure centers inside them Alphas did not. They were finely sensitive along the top wall, of course, and the prostate, but also the bottom and sides. The sensitivity and pleasure increased as the walls were stimulated through pressure and stroking. An Alpha knot should be pleasurable for Omegas, but it remained to be seen for damaged ones like Holland.

I continued to stroke him, moving my fingers in and out. He began to move his hips a little, back and forth for a minute. His hips gave a little swirl.

"You like it," I commented.

"I hate it because it's so good."

That made me smile, though my concern for him would never vanish. Not in this position.

"I'm ready," he declared a few seconds later, head coming up and body turning fast, then pushing me against my chest until I toppled backward onto the pillows and blankets.

His thighs rubbed against mine as he straddled me, moving up along my body, dragging his ass against my cock, his knees poking against my hips.

My body jerked in pleasure. My cock bobbed up and he caught it, giving it a few good strokes that made me tilt my head back and press hard into the pillow.

"Look at me," he commanded, haughty, himself again, chin high. He gave me a wry grin and curled his fingers tight about the base of my cock, holding me as he lowered himself over it.

I rocked my chin forward and watched him, the dark, slim feral boy in my bed, sheets of glossy hair pitching forward into his eyes and scraping his cheeks, eyes like pinpoints of dark-blue light pinning me into submission.

I felt the tip of my cock against his loose and open hole slip into his heat, passing the rigid muscles which gripped me with fine and measured strength.

His face contorted once, and for that moment I thought he would stop.

But he kept going and I slid right into him to the hilt.

I let out a pinched yell as the fires of utter bliss surrounded me.

Chapter Twenty-One

Holland

I loved the feel of his cock going into me. And because of the past I hated it. But I was no longer thinking of the past as my inner channel quivered in pleasure. I took the top position, which I always preferred with Ori, and controlled every aspect of this act. This union. This lovemaking.

My own cock pointed up, rigid and long, and waved up and down as I began to move.

It was awkward at first so I leaned forward, my hands on Ori's chest, to get my balance. He reached up and ran his hands down my arms, his eyes never leaving mine.

"Watch me." My voice husky. Shivery.

"I cannot take my eyes off you. You're gorgeous," he said.

I grinned down at him, inching slowly up off his big, sweet cock, my muscles milking it, pulling, tugging. I waited for the pain. It didn't come.

Slowly, I let myself back down. I worked him that way for about ten thrusts before my own slickness mixed with the lube he'd used and the passage inside me became easier and easier to take him.

Now it was good. Really good. My own cock wanted to be inside him, but for this—the mate-bond—it had to be this way. He had to knot me, fill me, pulse inside me until he was dry. I needed to be fully mated.

It was the true and right thing for us.

I thrilled at the prospect. I would be forever free of my past. I would be forever Ori's, even if never a free Omega.

The thought did not deter me. To be Ori's until we both stopped breathing a hundred or more years from now? Such a hardship.

My grin widened as I began to move faster.

Ori grunted and his hips jerked in response. He couldn't help it, I knew, but I put my hands on his waist to still him.

"Calm," I said. "Let me."

His eyes rolled up at my words, and I realized he really did get off on my domination.

We were perfect for each other.

His big hands wrapped about my thighs, inching to cup my buttocks as I moved upon him.

"Touch me more," I commanded.

He stroked my ass as I moved, kneading, gripping.

"Oh fuck!" It was so good I was on the verge of coming. Fast.

His hips bucked once more. His head came up and banged back on the pillow, mouth opening.

Faster and faster I rode him. One of his hands came around to stroke me and that was it. I went over the edge and my cock spurted hard, ribbons of white tossing themselves upon his chest.

So good. Better than good. Ecstasy of the best vintage because it was mixed with love, impossible to bottle, priceless if you ever could manage to sell it.

His cock swelled inside me as he began to come and the warmth of him began to fill me.

I continued to milk him with my muscles, pressing down on him as far as I could because I knew what was coming. The knot.

My body felt the widening of him at the base of his cock. So it began.

I pressed harder. I didn't want him to slip out now.

I felt it grow and swell, pressing my entrance. My heart leaped in my chest, unsure. But I kept pushing and he kept yelling as his orgasm swept him over and over.

Alphas were lucky that way. Prolonged coming. Fuck, I envied that. Multiple orgasms wracked them during a knot until they depleted everything they had to give.

He flooded my insides. I could already feel some of it leaking out of me, wetting the base of his cock. Before we were finished, it would drench us both, balls and all.

I'd seen Ori's knot before. He'd knotted with me inside him twice in all the times we made love. I'd squeezed it as I fucked him into bliss, a bulge that moved from the base of the cock and up the shaft, slowly, a thing of beauty and pleasure, a quivering, throbbing ball that swelled upward as it was stroked.

It made the skin of his dark cock shine where it stretched him. It made the tip of his cock bulge with pressure as it kept leaking, the little orifice growing redder and redder with the effort of expulsion.

This night I wouldn't see it but I was surely feeling it.

I stopped rocking and pressed my palms flat to his chest.

His breathing came fast. In gasps, he spoke through his throes of pleasure. "Holland, are you all right? I want—I want--"

I shut my eyes, feeling the way the knot burned a bit as it stretched and strained against my opening. The sting of it began but would pass as it moved.

"I'm all right. Hold me tight. I want to be yours." Carefully, I leaned toward him, opening my eyes.

He lay with his curls splashed against the pillow and his dark eyes shining.

"I won't hurt you. I swore it!" he breathed.

"You aren't hurting me. I want you. I want forever with you!"

We were both so young, but intrinsically I knew the truth of my words—*forever with you*—went beyond those three magical ones—I love you. This was more than a marriage. If it took, it would be a pure and true mate-bond, which meant I would feel his every Burn. I would feel the pull as if verbally called to his side. I would service him forever even at the expense of my own life.

Well, I loved the intent, but certainly I was not planning to die. Nor, I knew, was he.

His arms wrapped around my waist, fingers slipping on my hot skin. I felt the knot move, then, and the pressure against my hole gave a bit, and the sting receded.

I breathed and leaned into him, chest to chest, feeling him lock into me.

We stayed connected without effort now as his hips bucked in continuous pleasure and I held him through orgasm after orgasm. I kissed his neck, his chin, his jaw and finally, as he tilted his head down to me, his lush lips. Our tongues entwined.

I felt as if all barriers were stripped away. I lost all sense of where my skin ended and his began. The cock inside me became my cock, hard and pulsing as, to my great surprise, I felt myself come again.

Everything ceased to have any meaning but the two of us together, fitting like pieces of a puzzle meant to be interlocked to create an edge of a picture we could both only barely see at this point. But that puzzle was as big as life, and we were starting it together.

I felt an electric current run through my body and I could sense him in my mind now, a presence warm and lingering, something I wanted to grab with my thoughts as well as my limbs, and hold on never to let go.

I didn't actually hear Ori's thoughts, but I sensed his ecstasy, and his essence wove through me in a series of beautiful designs like elaborate braids and weavings and knots.

The knot inside me moved again, causing him to cry out into our kiss.

I rocked my hips, squeezed my muscles and milked him internally until the knot rose and rose, filling me with its pleasure and his seed.

Everything was wet: the air, our bodies, the sheets. It didn't matter. This was all.

Time stood still. I wanted the sensations within me to never end. But when I felt him jerk again in ecstasy, the knot deflated. My body sagged against him.

It was done.

I lifted my head. Our eyes met. But I didn't need to look at him to feel him in me now, mind and blood and bone. I knew the mate-bond had worked. It coursed in waves of longing and love I could barely contain.

"Oh wow," he said.

"Fuck. Yeah." I tried to shrug but I was already laughing at myself for trying to be an ass again. My old rude self.

I pulled my body up and off him, looking down at our wet bodies.

"Shower," I said. "New sheets."

"I know it's a mess," he began.

"Let's be quick."

His eyebrows went up.

I smacked him lightly on the shoulder "So we can do it all over again."

He sat up as I backed off him, but grabbed me hard, kissing me. When he pulled back, I said, "It's here." I pointed to my temple.

"I feel it." His smile cast its light all over me, making me hot again.

"I love you," I said.

He pushed me to the foot of the bed, slid off the edge, came around and picked me up as if I weighed no more than a bundle of feathers.

"I love you," he replied.

Like a man who'd won the grandest prize in a great battle, he carried me off to the shower.

It was like being drugged. I felt his Burn within me like a flame licking all along the insides of my skin.

When we emerged from the bathroom, clean once more, we changed the sheets, then tumbled into them to make love again.

We repeated that routine six more times before hunger drove us out of the room the next day. Plus, we'd run out of sheets.

Ori's Burn lasted two days and when he was cool again, and the extreme urgency left us, we went to his office and together filed our mate-bond status.

A nurse came to the house to take our blood.

After another two days, we got the results. Mate-bond status confirmed. Rating: Ten.

Epilogue

Orion

Holland spread my legs and dove between my thighs. He prepped me expertly for his favorite position to take me: face to face. His lips grazed my balls and cock. He licked and kissed the tip until I yelled. His fingers pushed in and out of my hole.

Lately, his presence in my mind swelled and burst with scents of honey and fresh flowers. He finally lined himself up and penetrated me, leaning over me, and his skin was the scent of spring and soap and new leaves.

He was pregnant six months now. He said he hated it, but he was always smiling, and his skin had taken on a golden glow. He was still slim and coltish, so his bump was small and round and barely bothered him, though he complained loud and often.

The day we found out we had made a child during the formation of our mate-bond, he said to me, "Do you wish for an Alpha?"

The words stung me with his pain. He had been through so much, and though we were happy, our Alpha-ruled world had a long way to go to make it safe and equal for Omegas.

"I wish for a child as beautiful and brilliant as you are. And if he's Omega, we'll raise him together to be strong and proud. We will give him everything."

He blinked for a moment, the rims of his eyes going a little red. He did not reply except to wrap his arms around my shoulders and press himself against me.

Now I kissed the top of his head, my lips in his hair, as he bent to thrust into me and take his pleasure as he wished, as I wished him to take it.

I'd been through two more Burns during his pregnancy. His strength never faltered. He took me hard, as I liked it, and when my knots formed he used his hands to keep me in that prolonged state of bliss.

He told me once that he hated I could knot and he couldn't.

I said, "Use our bond. You can feel it."

"Oh, I most certainly do feel it," he replied.

I learned to be an excellent lover and give him as many orgasms in a night as he could stand.

Now he rocked into me and our usual merging of body and mind began with the electric currents racing through our bodies and our minds. We were so attuned we groaned in unison and came together. As we always did.

I loved him more than I ever thought I could love another.

We rested side by side in our bed, our legs tangled, our breaths one.

"I decided on a name," he said, his hand stroking up and down my side. "For him."

He pressed his swollen belly to my belly. With our strong bond, I could almost feel the child growing inside me as well.

"It's taken you long enough."

"I know. But now I'm sure."

"What is it?"

"Xavier," he said. "It means new beginning."

"It's perfect." I leaned toward him. Our lips met. Our minds ached with a new need to merge.

I chuckled against his mouth.

He put his hand on the center of my chest. "On your back again," he said, and the smile he gave me was old and new at the same time, showing me all of him, where he came from, what he had suffered, and how happy he was now. It was filled with the burning of our love combined.

THE END

Contact links for Wendy Rathbone:

Join my Facebook group Wendyland. I post updates, cover reveals, snippets, sales and other fun stuff every day: https://www.facebook.com/groups/718074255203918/

Friend me on Facebook: https://www.facebook.com/wendy.rathbone.3

Follow my Amazon author page: https://www.amazon.com/Wendy-Rathbone/e/B00B0O9BMS/ref=dp_byline_cont_ebooks_1

Follow me on Bookbub: https://www.bookbub.com/authors/wendy-rathbone

Dear Reader:

Thank you for reading **The Alpha's Fake Mate: The Omega Misfits Book 2**.

I so loved writing about these characters as well as making the cover. Holland was a special joy for me. Every word from him in the book was a pleasure to write. Though I love all my characters, he stood out for me more than most!

Next on my agenda is book 3 in *The Omega Misfits* series: **The Alpha and the Sylph.** Finally you will get to see the unhappy fate of Sylphs, but one Sylph in particular, Misha, breaks all the odds. Born without the disabilities most Sylphs endure, he tells his story of discovery, finding wholeness in his life, and finally love. I hope you come along with me on this journey of continuing my discovery of this omegaverse I have created.

Happy Reading!

Love,
Wendy Rathbone

About Wendy Rathbone

Read Wendy Rathbone... where imposters and outcasts, princes and lost boys always find their happily every after.

I have written in all genres: sci-fi, fantasy, horror, paranormal, contemporary, erotica, romance. But I keep coming back to romance as the main focus. Gay romance. Male/male romance. The idea of two men falling in love is irresistible to me. It's all I write now.

All my books are available on Amazon and most are in Kindle Unlimited. So if you have the urge, go take a look. See what's on the shelf.

Male/male romance books by Wendy:

The Kingdom of Slaves Series
  (contemporary fantasy mm romance)

The Slave Palace
The Slave Harem
Master of Halloween (short story)
The Secret Slave (coming sometime 2020)

The Omega Misfits
  (Omegaverse mm romance)

Trust No Alpha
The Alpha's Fake Mate
The Alpha and the Sylph (coming April 2020)

The Imposter Series (fantasy mm romance)

The Imposter Prince
The Imposter King

The Moonling Prince Series
(fantasy, sci fi mm romance)

The Moonling Prince
The Coming of the Light

The Foundling Series
(contemporary billionaire mm romance trilogy)

Rescue Me
Sacrifice Me
Remember Me

The Fantastic Immortals Series
(fantasy/myth mm romance)

Ganymede: Abducted by the Gods
Zeus: Conquering his Heart

Stand Alone Novels

Sci Fi MM Romance

Solstice Gift (holiday)
Not Another Hero
Cocky Virgin Prince
Prey
Scoundrel
The Android and the Thief
   (Second edition coming spring 2020)
Letters to an Android

Fantasy MM Romance

<u>Lord Vampyre</u>
<u>Lace</u>
<u>Snow of the White Hills</u> (mm fairy tale)
<u>The Elves of Christmas</u> (holiday fantasy mm romance)

Contemporary MM Romance

<u>Romantically Incorrect</u>
<u>Snowfall and Romance</u> (Christmas novel)
<u>The Bodyguard's Valentine</u>
<u>Buying You</u>

TRUST NO ALPHA
Wendy Rathbone

It's a world gone mad. The Alphas are out of control.

When you discover you're not who you thought you were, the nightmare begins.

KRIS

At age eighteen, life as he knows it is over for Kris. A secret to his nature he was not aware of has been revealed.

Now, kept as a prisoner in a locked room in the mansion of his wealthy father, Kris is at the mercy of Alpha laws and Alpha domination.

Things take a turn for the worse when his own litter mate threatens him, and his father starts behaving strangely around him.

Escape is his only hope. But where can he go in a world that allows him no rights?

THORNE

Marked as a dangerous Alpha, and living a secluded life alone and unloved, Thorne still grieves for the mate whose death he feels responsible for.

Years have passed, and he refuses to even try to function in normal society.

One day he discovers a young man on his property, disheveled, desperate, and scared. He acts like a runaway Omega, but he doesn't smell like one.

What is this boy? And why does Thorne feel an immediate need to protect him? To bond him? To make him his?

A non-shifter, Omegaverse love story of rescue, first time, fertility issues and an HEA. Standalone read. 65,500 words. (While Omegas are birth-fathers in this universe, there is no on-page mpreg in this book.)

SNOWFALL AND ROMANCE
Wendy Rathbone

A blizzard. A Christmas rescue. A man with the heart of an angel.

Hayden - Hayden knows it was stupid to think he could walk home from the office and beat the blizzard. So what if he worked out all the time until he was big and strong. So what if he hated to ever ask for help. Loners who think they can do everything themselves are just as vulnerable as anyone. His only consolation is if he dies there will be very few people who will miss him.

Matthew - The half-frozen man falling through the door to Matthew's coffee shop is more than alarming, but it's a good thing he'd forgotten to lock that front entrance or the beautiful guy covered in snow might have died in the cold.

The man is gorgeous, soft-spoken, helpful, maybe even a bit old-fashioned in his manners. Just the type Matthew always wished for but never met. Sharing a fire and a snowed-in night with him will be no hardship.

When the storm lasts more than a day, attraction blooms. But when it is over, will Hayden and Matthew's feelings fade? Or will holiday charm and a heart-warming miracle draw them together again?

Rescue, forced proximity, overwhelming attraction, blizzards, and a heart-warming Christmas miracle. Although this book is part of *A Snow Globe Christmas* series, it is a complete stand alone and it isn't a requirement that you read the previous books to follow along. We wish everyone a happy holiday.

216

THE SLAVE PALACE
Wulf and Locke
WENDY RATHBONE

Conquered. Captured. Sold as a pleasure slave.

After being taken as a prisoner of war, Wulf fights his captors and is sold as a One-Night Thrall to be used and abused, then put to death. He is purchased by a high ranking master of the famous Slave Palace. Why Locke buys him, Wulf has no clue, but something about this master is intriguing. Instead of abuse, Wulf is plied with luxuries he has never known by a man who actually seems to respect him.

Jaded. Looking for a challenge.

Eminent Master Locke takes on a bet with his best friend that he can't train and tame a dangerous One-Night Thrall in ten days. But something about this slave stirs him like no other before. All bets aside, Locke has the urge to keep Wulf, as well as save his life. But Wulf is fierce, unwilling, and his consent papers have been forged. If Wulf doesn't soon submit to his role as a slave, he will be sent to death as a prisoner of war.

A sweet, slow-burn love story taking place on an alternate contemporary Earth where owning pleasure slaves is legal.

LORD VAMPYRE
Wendy Rathbone

When Lord Neverelle becomes a guest at Cliffside Keep, Vanni watches helplessly as Damion, the young man he's grown up with and secretly loves, falls for the alluring and seductive stranger. Lord Neverelle is danger incarnate, and soon takes control of the household.

Not satisfied with Damion alone, Never uses a vampire trick called "the tempt" to compel Vanni, who is swept into a love triangle that includes fiery passion and nightly threesomes.

Now Vanni must ask himself, is any of this consensual? And what about Damion—does he really want to be with Vanni, or is it all a sensual play controlled by vampire compulsion?

M/M and M/M/M romance.

The Imposter Prince
Book 1 in The Imposter Series
Wendy Rathbone

His love for an enemy prince threatens his very life.

Dare does not mind serving the spoiled and cruel Prince Darius. Growing up with him, Dare does everything for Darius including homework, bed play demands, and even doubling for him as the prince grows too paranoid to face even the smallest of crowds.

But everything changes in a single moment when Dare, while posing as Darius, is abducted by the enemy.

A captive in a new and hostile land, Dare meets another prince who seems just as indulged and rotten as Darius—until Dare gets to know him, until they fall in love. Against his will, Dare must continue to play the role of Prince Darius for real, or risk everything: his love, his land, and his very life.

His only chance for survival is to keep a secret from the one he loves, a secret that is also killing him.

A male/male, enemies to lovers novel of mad kings, troubled princes, abduction, fevers, cold dungeons, warm hearths, comfort, wine, and true love.

Ganymede: Abducted by the Gods
Book 1 in "The Fantastic Immortals" Series (A standalone read)
Wendy Rathbone

My name is Ganymede, and I have been betrayed.

Every boy my age dreams of leaving home to embark on a noble adventure, but never does any boy imagine it happening as it did to me. On the evening of my 18th naming day, when I expected no more than a chalice of wine and a few drunken flirtations to tempt my innocence, I was instead sold by my father to the god, Zeus - not because of anything particular I had ever done or said, but solely because I am considered beautiful among mortals, and my father found more value in a few gold coins than in the well-being of his youngest son.

To be honest, I never believed in the gods, but my lack of belief held no power in Olympus or on Earth. Now under Zeus's influence, I am kept drunk on ambrosia in the sun-lit halls of the immortals, alternately amazed and horrified at the power these beings hold over others, and how darkly they influence the progress of humanity itself. How very much I want to hate Zeus for kidnapping me, and yet he shows me mostly kindness, even on that fateful night when we shared a bed for the first time. Kindness, yes, but also a godly and unyielding refusal to take no for an answer... probably because he could read my ambrosia-fevered curiosity as much as my naive, inexperienced terror. He owns me, after all, just as he owns everything else, so perhaps it never occurred to him that a captive and a slave might not make the best of lovers.

Throughout my time at Olympus - who's to say how long I've been here, for time on Olympus is not the same as that on Earth - the only thing that gives me hope comes to me in dreams and visions. His name is Sable and he is a magnificent shape-shifter in the form of a giant raven. When he first spoke to me in my mind it was with a resonance unlike any I had ever known - his mind and mine sounding a single note together, a song without words, a promise of freedom, a glimpse of some distant but very real possibility of this thing we humans call Love. But now he is silent. Perhaps I dreamed his voice. Perhaps I have finally lost my mind.

ZEUS (Conquering His Heart)
Book 2 in "The Fantastic Immortals" Series
(A standalone read)
WENDY RATHBONE

When I throw the lightning and summon the thunder, it isn't always out of anger, but often from a love so all-consuming it could only be the effect of Eros himself. Yes, he is beautiful. Of course he is. How could he be otherwise, with hair the color of sunlight and white-feathered wings that drape to the floor? And he is as ancient as the myth of time itself, an immortal with powers and glamour beyond my ability to imagine. He struggles to teach me wisdom, control, strategy, yet I sit here babbling like a child, for all I can think of is how I might try - at least let me try! - to prove myself to him in some way that will cause him to crave my company and my touch, just as I crave his.

I do not yet know how to be a god, for I am only 18 and still just a silly boy who has fallen in love with Love himself, while my father Cronus plots and schemes to lock me in his dungeon and make me his slave forever.

A male/male romance.

BUYING YOU
Wendy Rathbone

It's one thing to be a beautiful cover model on billboards, buses and magazine covers. It's quite another to be sold as one.

Prized for his looks, Dane knows it's shallow, but he is on his way to having it all. It feels good to be gorgeous, smart and have top designers from around the world requesting him.

When he returns to his hometown to participate in a small Date-For-Charity auction, it seems harmless enough—until a hooded man walks in and bids higher on him than anyone else. Dane is intrigued but nervous when he finds out the guy has vanished after the winning bid, leaving only a limo behind to whisk Dane off into the night.

Enemies to lovers, opposites attract, and hot steamy nights that challenge two guys' trust issues along with their biggest fears.

The Foundling, Rescue Me (Book 1)
Wendy Rathbone

What do you do when you find an unconscious man floating on a raft in the middle of the Caribbean? Rescue and fall in love with him, of course!

Well, that's not me! I'm a businessman first and foremost with an underworld reach that stretches from my island all the way to Miami. I'm too busy to rescue strays. I have no time for lovers. And I don't fall in love.

But Alec is beautiful, vulnerable, and my heart won't stop pounding. My every waking thought is of him. I can't concentrate. The world is suddenly vibrant and colorful. Flowers assault me with their sweet fragrance. Food tastes fresher. And my body is hot, so hot all the time.

I have done some dark deeds in my life and cared little for their affects on others as long as they gained me everything I sought. But now... one good deed and I don't know who I am anymore.

Billionaire, organized crime, amnesia, hurt/comfort, tropical hot-hot, happy for now. Book one of the Foundling trilogy. (Previously published under the title "The Foundling," this book is a newly edited, updated edition.)

The Foundling, Sacrifice Me (Book 2)

What do you do when your beautiful new lover's life is in danger and he wants to be bait to catch the enemy? You protect him with all your might.

Alec is still trying to remember who he is and is haunted by terrible nightmares. Diego is being investigated for murder. Their chemistry grows hotter and stronger even as Diego's ex, Sasha, comes for a visit and looking for a job.

Who can they trust to help them? Enemies are everywhere and the jungle closes in.

The Foundling, Remember Me (Book 3)

What do you do when your memories return and the most horrific nightmare you can imagine is real?

You try to bury it. You try to run. But none of that works.

Your lover is rock solid. He is always there for you, but is it enough?

Diego and Alec now live under witsec in San Francisco, thousands of miles away from the Caribbean. But their past still haunts them.

Alec is beginning to remember who he really is, but reliving the torment he went through threatens to destroy his sanity. Is Diego's love enough to hold onto such a broken man?

SONS OF NEVERLAND
A Deliciously Dark Male/Male Romance
Della Van Hise

Set against a backdrop of contemporary culture, *Sons of Neverland* explores the universal questions of love, sex and death - the three most crucial challenges every human being must face.

Stefan London is a grieving man, suffering through the loss of his young daughter. When he goes to a science fiction convention in the hopes of meeting her friends, he encounters instead a man who is dangerously seductive. Lured into the night, Stefan soon discovers himself in a world where vampires are real, and immortality is only a kiss away.

But the price of eternal life is high, and as his handsome maker warns, "Through my blood you will learn a secret that will compel you to live forever, yet a secret so sinister it will haunt you for that same eternity."

The secret will haunt you, too.

YEAR OF THE RAM
Della Van Hise

Year of the Ram was described by one reviewer as... "A space-faring gay romance full of love, angst, and longing."

Only after Star Commander Morgan Diego becomes an exile as a result of a Galaxy Corps political blunder does he begin to realize how much he valued the companionship of his second in command - the mysterious Lucien, an Alfarian who is more elfen than human, with peculiar powers and abilities which begin to unfold as he, too, realizes what he has lost.

Separated by circumstance from his former life, Morgan is thrust into a world where he must survive by his wits. When he meets a peculiar little old man calling himself Kim Le, Morgan finds himself in a situation where he is required to master The Art - not only a form of human & extraterrestrial martial arts, but a way of living that will alter his life forever.

At the temple, he is introduced to his new teacher, another Alfarian man who begins to steal his heart - a heart which is already promised to Lucien. Torn and conflicted, Morgan struggles with the world he left behind and the world he now inhabits.

Beginning to believe he may never again return to his ship and to the friends and loved ones he left behind, he is all the more frustrated and heartbroken when a new Master arrives at the temple: a man to whom Morgan is immediately drawn both mentally and physically, a man who is strikingly familiar... yet utterly alien.

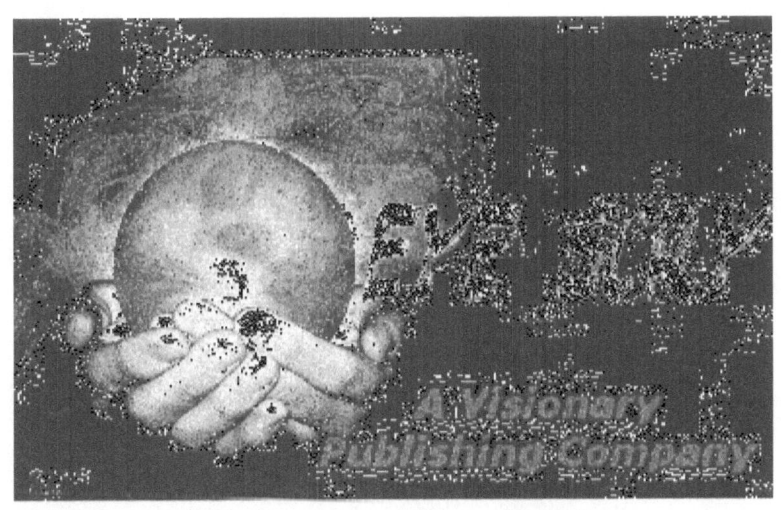

Eye Scry Publications
A Visionary Publishing Company

www.ingramcontent.com/pod-product-compliance
Lightning Source LLC
Chambersburg PA
CBHW032046240626
47154CB00003B/1099